The King Never Dies

Gary Greenwood

RazorBlade Press

The King Never Dies

This book was first published in 2001 by
RazorBlade Press, 108 Habershon St, Splott,
Cardiff,
CF24 2LD

The King Never Dies is a work of fiction.
The characters and events described are imaginary and
any resemblance to people living or dead is purely
coincidental.

Designed and typeset by
RazorBlade Press

Printed and bound by the Guernsey Press.

British Library in Publication Data.
A catalogue record for this book is available
from the British Library

ISBN 0-9531468 9 8

Gary Greenwood

<u>Dedications/Acknowledgements</u>

this one is for the future:

Christopher David William Bull, Emma Diana Holly
Bull, Benjamin William Hayward,
Joshua Harley Hollister, Eleanor Rose Lebbon,
Lily Mae O'Hagan,
Mary Nancy O'Hagan, Lukas Christopher William
Rogers,
Seren May Elizabeth Thomas-Wilcox

here's hoping they make a better job of it than we will

Alphabetical acknowledgements are also due to the following:

Chris Nurse for the excellent covers
Darren Floyd for having the guts to publish me again
Darren Wilcox for this book's unofficial subtitle
Everyone at Newport Job Centre for all their support
Lil and Cath for doing so much with Spread The Word
II

    Ly Rand for getting past the Bishops to get the photos of the Spitalfields interior
Mark Chadbourn for inviting me to the "World's End"
Matt Williams and Max O'Hagan for being, as much as it pains me to say it, basically insane
Simon Clark for his kind words and encouragement
Spike for the info about Hawksmoor and Christchurch and for getting me on the net (eventually!)
Tim Lebbon for his unending support and ginger comments

And I will give unto thee
the keys of the kingdom
of heaven: and whatso-
ever thou shalt bind on
earth shall be bound in
heaven: and whatsoever
thou shalt loose on
earth shall be loosed in
heaven.

    Matthew, Ch 16, v 19

Chapter One

Since the Godhead had appeared, the world had gone to Hell.

It was a Saturday night in November. That was when everything started to go wrong for me.

The pub was crowded with the usual mix of students, out for as much beer as they could afford on their measly loans, and regulars, who sat at the bar and viewed the interlopers with drunken and self-righteous disdain. Jerry and I had to fight to get to the bar, pushing through the sticky crowd of people, everyone around us shouting into someone else's ear to be heard above the roar of conversation combined with screaming of the too-loud jukebox. What little lighting there was in the place was filtered through the smoke of hundreds of cigarettes, the blue clouds moving slowly within the pale lights, twirling and twisting above their creators, mimicking their lazy dance moves. The only vacant space in the entire place was around one table where three Downers sat, their skin cracked and blistered, flashes of red showing through the blackened skin when they smiled like glimpses of lava beneath a volcano's surface. The heat they radiated, as well as their appearance and reputation, kept everyone a respectful distance from them as they sat and talked. The table harbored scorch marks from where their hands had rested a little too long, and their suits and ties smouldered gently.

We finally managed to get served and, clutching our pints, walked away from the bar and general dancing area, eventually muscling our way next to a pillar. As we leaned against it, Jerry winced and took a pistol from inside his jacket, laying it on the shelf next to his pint. Lighting a cigarette and offering one to him, I noticed a few people glance at us, or more accurately at Jerry's piece, before they turned back to their friends.

"What the hell did you bring that for?" I asked him. He smiled and shrugged.

"You never know," he said, sipping at his beer. "You heard the latest?" I had to lean in towards him to hear the words that were spat out in a plume of smoke. I shook my head. It had been a long time since I had heard any news ,

5

whether domestic, foreign or even just gossip. "The Arch-bishop of Canterbury's dead," he said simply. I raised an eyebrow at him and asked him how it had happened. Jerry shrugged. "How do you think? The Godhead did it,"

"You're kidding?" It was Jerry's turn to shake his head.

"Nope. Well, it probably wasn't the Godhead himself, you know, but he must have ordered it. They found him this morning, crucified in Canterbury Cathedral on a big wooden cross. You know Jesus had INRI posted above his head?" He pronounced the initials as one word, *inree*. "I can't remember the Latin but it stood for Jesus of Nazareth, King of the Jews, yeah? Well the Archbishop apparently had D.F.W.M. above his." This time he spelt out the initials, but it didn't help me any.

"What does it stand for?" I asked.

"No one seems to know for sure. The news has been coming up with all sorts of Latin phrases, but word is - " he grinned, savouring the punch-line, "- it stands for Don't Fuck With Me!" Jerry laughed and took a drink, glancing around at the people nearby, staring at the girls, both the students and the better-dressed crowd, and licked his lips free of the foam from his beer. I nudged his arm and motioned for him to carry on. "What can I say? He'd obviously had enough of the old guy. Had him crucified and left to be found. Some sort of press release was issued saying he'd been a false prophet,"

"That's original," I said. The archbishop had been in his seventies at least and, since he'd taken over the job just before the troubles, had seemed to try his best to provide some form of assistance to the faithful. And not just Christians, I remembered, thinking of his historic visit to Israel where he had been shown blessing the victims of the latest attacks, al-though not in a strictly denominational sense; it had been a message from the heart, a demonstration of the empathy of an old man for those who had suffered and would suffer even more. At least, that was how it had seemed to me at the time, but then times had changed.

Jerry nudged me and pointed towards the bar. We watched the crowd part like the proverbial Red Sea as one of the Downers strode to the bar, holding the three empty glasses used by himself and his two friends. While the conversation didn't exactly die, it became muted; people were afraid of these strange beings and had no idea how to act around them, except to obey their basic instincts and avoid them. The Downer, like most of his kind, was small and compact, his obligatory black suit tight across his chest and shoulders, his body emitting faint wisps of steam which drifted lazily up to mix with the cigarette smoke. While Jerry and I had waited for close on fifteen minutes to be served, the Downer had obviously been seen coming and by the time he reached the bar, three fresh pints stood waiting for him. He smiled, his face cracking open around his lips and cheeks; even from where I stood, I could see a thin trickle of red leak from one of the gaps and drip on to his jacket, joining the other splashes of colour that had solidified like droplets of wax on the material. He handed a ten-pound note to the barmaid, the edges crisp and brown, then picked up his change from where she placed it on the bar. No one wanted to touch a Downer. The crowd parted again as he carefully walked back to his table holding the three pints in front of him.

"Creepy fuckers, ain't they?" Jerry said as the level of conversation returned to its usual frantic height, words seeming to float up to the ceiling only to be choked by the smoke that lay in wait. "The Archbishop of Canterbury's dead and those bastards are still around."

I grunted as I quickly finished up my pint, and waited until Jerry finished his. "Another?" I asked him, pointing to his glass. "Sure," he said. I took both empties and, cigarette in mouth, smoke trailing over my shoulder, went to the bar.

I stood behind two rows of people, all of us waiting our turn to slip into the gap left by somebody else as they turned away from the bar shouting "Excuse me!", holding their drinks in front of and above them like a priest at communion. Slowly, one by one, the men and women standing at the bar trickled to the front and, about ten minutes after I joined the crowd, I rested our glasses and my elbows on the beer-soaked towels and tried to catch the eye of one of the four barmaids.

As always, it's the heat that you notice first. The fast build-up of heated air circulating around you, warming your body as it surrounds you like a suffocating cushion, hot and sticky, tinged with the tart smells that come from the Downers' bodies. Then there's the drop in sound, the level of conversation falling off like ice melting before the onset of a summer breeze, as the squat figure sidles into view. Glancing sideways, I saw him put a black hand on the rail at the bar, the skin crackling audibly as his fingers bent around the brass tube, steam rising from the contact a second or two later.

"What can I get you?" the barmaid asked the Downer. He opened his mouth to order something, his other hand already reaching into his pocket for his change when someone said, "Hey! I was here first,"

It was me.

The Downer looked over at me. His eyes, like those of all Downers, were crimson, with occasional tears of blood-red lava trickling from the corners to either fall on to his clothing or be reabsorbed into the blasted landscape of his face. He grinned, his skin splitting, oozing red before it sealed itself again almost instantly, leaving a new scar amongst thousands of others. The heat from his body was like that of a furnace; the posters that hung from the bar advertising beers flapped madly as the rush of hot air soared upwards. He took his hand from the rail leaving a faint burnished imprint on the metal.

"I'm sorry. Please, buy your drinks first," the Downer said, indicating the bar. Around me, with the jukebox still and quiet between songs, the only sound was the scuttling of whispers, running from one person to another as they watched the show before them. I turned slightly to face the barmaid, who stood unsure of what to do. I smiled confidently and was about to order two pints when the back of my neck blazed in agony as the Downer grabbed me, pushing my face down on to the bar. His hand felt like a scabrous hot water bottle, recently filled straight from the kettle, pressing down on me. "You fucker!" he hissed, pushing his face close to mine, his steaming breath almost making my eyelashes curl. "Fuck do you think you're doing?"

My hand reached into my jeans pocket, curling around both my keys. I formed a fist, the metal sticking out from between my fingers, and pulled my arm back, planning to punch the son of a bitch in the gut if I couldn't reach his face, when he let go. Somebody pulled me backwards, away from the burnt man, and I spun, my fist full of keys ready. "Hey! It's me!" Jerry said, grabbing my hand before I could do any damage. We glanced at the Downer, who stood talking calmly with another of his kind, wearing the same sort of suit and tie. He and the first one laughed at some privately shared joke, ignoring me completely, as three packets of peanuts and a pint arrived on the bar for them. As they moved away, I staggered against Jerry, the pain from the back of my neck washing over me suddenly. "Hey, whoa, whoa there," he said, clutching me under my armpits and holding me up. "Come on, let's get out of here and get that sorted."

"No, I'm okay," I managed to say, supporting my own weight again. I leaned against a fruit machine that guaranteed a top pay-out of a massive five pounds, and watched as the Downer and his friend walked away, over to the others at their table. "Who the fuck was that?" I asked, reaching around gingerly to touch the raw and blistered skin of my neck. The collar of my jacket had taken the worst of the attack; when I brought my hand back in front of me, I saw charred pieces of cloth were stuck to my fingers.

"Never mind who that was, we need to get something on that," Jerry said, stepping around me and pulling my collar down slightly. "Jesus, Aitch. You lost your fucking mind over the last five years or something?" he said as he looked at the damage. Around us, the other customers began to drift back into their own conversations, the floor show over as far as they were concerned.

"How bad is it?" I asked him.

"I've seen worse," he admitted, lighting up two cigarettes and offering me one of them to replace the one I'd dropped on the floor when my neck was being branded. "But I still reckon we ought to put something on it." His Zippo clicked open and I leaned forward to light my fag.

"Aitch, you bastard! How stupid are you to start something with a fucking Downer, man?" Jerry and I looked up to see the six-foot-two frame of Hal Hughes, his dark-skinned face broken up by a pearly white smile dotted with three gold teeth, and his head topped off by a ridiculous pink top knot that hung down to his shoulders. He held out his hand and took mine, pulling me towards him and hugging me, clapping me on the back, making me wince when my jacket moved against the blisters. "Jerry, how you doing, fella?" he said, shaking Jerry's hand before turning back to me. "How long you been back in town, man?"

"Couple of days," I replied, looking up at my old friend. We'd known each other for years, the pair of us living in what we'd called the Qizilbash Orphanage until we'd both escaped at thirteen and began to run loose about the big city, struggling to make a living. We had both had a modicum of success, Hal more than myself, and everything had seemed to be going well until five years ago; at the time I was involved in a situation which had serious repercussions and, as a result, had to leave this fair isle for a time.

"You're back here two days and already you're fucking with a Downer? Haven't you learned anything, man?" Hal said with a laugh. "Come on, I want you guys to meet an old friend. Should be able to put some shit on those fucking blisters, too." Jerry checked he had his pistol tucked in his inside pocket again then the pair of us followed Hal through the crowd, fortunately away from the Downers' table.

In one corner, separated from the rest of the pub by a high wooden rail, was an area which could have served as a stage for bands to play upon. As it was, it was furnished with three sofas, two beneath a large frosted window that gave a distorted view of the world outside, the other with its back to the pub. A small table sat between them, its surface dotted with glasses, both empty and full. A gorilla in a tuxedo stood at the top of the three small steps that led up to the stage in front of the only opening in the railings. He stood aside as Hal, Jerry and I walked up, nodding politely at Hal and glaring at us. On one of the sofas below the window, his feet propped up on the table, sat a large coloured guy, a pair of small round spectacles sitting on his face; they somehow managed to look embarrassed at how out of place they looked on such a big man. One of the man's large, meaty arms was draped around the shoulders of an Oriental girl who nestled against him, her skirt far too short for the time of year. Another girl, wearing jeans and a sweater, sat on the other sofa, laughing and drinking with a tall, pale Upper dressed completely in black with matching sunglasses.

"Hey, Roller, you remember Aitch?" Hal asked the big coloured man. Roller smiled, then removed his arm from the girl's shoulders and stood, offering me his hand. "How are you?" he asked, his voice, like his glasses, out of place in such a big man; it was quiet and cultured, without any hint of a discernible accent. "This is his friend, Jerry," Hal said. Roller shook Jerry's hand.

"Please, sit down," Roller said. We sat opposite him, on the sofa with its back to the pub, while Hal sat on the seat with the pale man and the girl. "Would you like a drink?" We asked for two pints and, though no one left to order them, a barmaid stepped up to our table a few minutes later with our drinks.

"Aitch here's just had a bit of a run-in with one of those Downers," Hal said. "Show Roller your neck, man." Feeling slightly uncomfortable, I leaned forward, exposing my neck. I didn't see Roller make any gesture, but I presume he did so, because a moment later the Oriental girl sat next to me and pressed some cooling cloth against my skin.

"Keep that there for the next ten minutes or so," she said as I straightened up. The girl smiled and returned to her seat. Roller took a large cigar and lit it, puffing out plumes of smoke. Beside Hal, the Upper and his girl laughed quietly to themselves. "Aitch McKean. It's been a while," I nodded. Truth to tell, I'd only met Roller once before, when I'd been hanging out with Hal a few years back. "Are you now treading the righteous straight and narrow?" he asked, a grin revealing whiter-than white-teeth.

"I plan to stay out of trouble, that's for sure," I said.

"Seems like you haven't made the best possible start," he said through a cloud of cigar smoke. An uncomfortable, embarrassed pause in the conversation slipped quietly between us like a cat sneaking into a room, bringing with it the chill night air. I didn't know what to say, and I know damn well Jerry didn't either. With one hand holding the cold cloth against my neck, I lifted my pint to my lips with the other, my gaze darting around, looking at anyone and anything except the big guy opposite me.

Once again, there was the slight build-up of heat off to one side. I and everyone else turned to the steps that led up to the stage area. The tuxedoed gorilla stood in front of a Downer and another Upper, tall and thin, wearing sunglasses, jeans and a sleeveless T-shirt. Tattoos ran from his shoulders down to his wrists, a colourful medley of snakes with large teeth, dragons with big wings and women with huge breasts. For all his bulk and size, the bouncer was visibly sweating, and I don't think it was just from the heat. The Downer ignored him completely and stared directly at Roller.

"Good evening. I apologise if I am interrupting anything," he said, his voice smooth and mellow, carrying perfectly over the noise of the jukebox. "It seems an associate of mine would like a quiet word with one of your company." Though he didn't look at me, the Downer very slightly moved his hand, indicating me. Jerry and I glanced at each other. One of his hands slid into the inside of his jacket.

"Please, you're not interrupting anything," Roller said, as evenly as the Downer. "My friends and I were merely enjoying a few drinks and catching up on old times."

The Downer smiled and bowed his head slightly. The top of his head was much like his face — scorched and blackened, rivulets of red seeping through here and there. "May I request the audience of Mr McKean?" he asked. Shit, I thought, they know my name.

"I'm sorry, but Mr McKean and I have business to attend to. He will not be available for the rest of the evening," Roller said, puffing on his cigar. Around us, in the rest of the pub, everyone carried on as normal, drinking and dancing, smoking and snogging, oblivious to what was building up. The Downer's smile failed, the edges of his mouth dropping slowly, molten rock dripping over a precipice.

"I must insist, sir, that Mr McKean accompany me to my table," he stated, leaving no room for argument. The Tattooed Upper took the steps in one go, his hand lightly pushing aside the bouncer who remained motionless, unsure of what to do, how to handle the Downer and his friend. Jerry pulled his pistol from inside his jacket, bringing it level with the Tattooed Upper's midriff as he turned to me, his long-nailed hand reaching out to grasp my shoulder. With his other hand he pulled his sunglasses off and stared down, his eyes sunk deep in hollows, almost hypnotising me.

On the other sofa, the thin Upper in black coughed slightly. The Tattooed Upper glanced over at him, releasing me from his gaze, and then from his grip. Roller's friend shook his head, wagged his finger and tutted at the Tattooed Upper, smiling all the while. Without a word being spoken, my would-be kidnapper retreated down the steps and joined the Downer, who glared at us all in turn before they both walked away, leaving me shaking and sweating.

Roller looked over at me as Jerry put away his pistol. "So, Aitch, you're staying out of trouble, huh?" He reached into his top pocket and flicked a business card over to me. "Only way you're gonna do that is by working for me. I own you now."

I looked over at Hal. He shrugged, his pink topknot wobbling slightly. Jerry and I grabbed our drinks, downed them in one, said our thanks and left.

*

"What a great start to the fucking weekend," Jerry said as we walked home, our shoulders hunched against the light rain that was falling, a drizzle which would have been bearable were it not for the driving wind that sought out every gap in our clothing and slipped inside it like a lover with razor blades for fingers. "Not only have we got the Downers pissed off at us, but some gangster is on our case as well. Fucking great." Jerry always was one for the odd bout of self pity.

"Do you know who that guy in the shades was? The Upper who stopped the other one with the tattoos?" I asked him, searching for a non-existent packet of fags. Jerry noticed and reached into his pocket, handing me his. We stood still for a second.

"No idea. I hardly know Hal, let alone his mates," he said as I lit my cigarette, the flame bathing my face in an all too brief warm glow. "I've heard rumours, though," he said as we walked on, turning down a darkened street that led to his house.

"What sort of rumours?"

"There's a guy I know who works in the docks claims he knows Hal, does a bit of work for Roller, you know. He says the guy —"

"Gimme your money! Now!"

We turned at the sound of the voice. Stood in the entrance to a small alley that we had just strolled by, a large knife pointed at us, was a kid of fourteen or fifteen, wearing a hooded sweatshirt pulled up over his head to keep the rain off and a pair of dirty jeans above a worn-out pair of trainers. Jerry and I looked at each other slowly, grins spreading over our faces. After all we had been through — burned by a Downer, almost being kidnapped by a Downer and his spooky friend, then being drafted into working for a gangster — we were now being held up by a kid who was half our age. Jerry started chuckling first, quietly behind his hand, glancing at the kid as he stood in the rain, then I joined in, nervousness and the beer creasing us up until we were doubled over, laughing like a pair of idiots at the crazy kid who was trying to rob us.

The kid stepped forward and stabbed Jerry in the guts.

"Huh?" was all Jerry could say before he dropped to his knees, both of them cracking loudly on the pavement as he fell, the knife sliding out of him.

"No fucker laughs at me," the kid said.

I moved without thinking, reflexes taking over. In one second I was next to the kid, his knife hand in one of mine, his collar in the other. He just had time to register surprise before I head-butted him, his nose squashing beneath my forehead, the blood spurting down his face as he made an "Ack!" noise in the back of his throat. I pulled back and kicked him hard in the balls, still holding his knife hand as he doubled over, only to be met by my knee slamming into his face on its way down. He jerked upright again, blood spraying up in an arc from his ruined features as he bounced off my knee, only to have my fist slam into his neck, smashing into his Adam's apple. With a contemptuous snort, I released his arm and watched as he slid down the wall, until he sat slumped on the ground.

I turned to Jerry to ask how he was doing. He was still on his knees, but he'd straightened up, one hand clutching his belly which even in the dark looked wet, too wet for the rain to be the cause. In the other hand he held his pistol. I managed to say "No" without any real conviction then jumped as he squeezed the trigger, shooting the mugger in the head, spraying what little brains the kid had over the floor in an explosion of sound and light. The recoil sent Jerry falling on to his back, his own head smacking the tarmac of the road with a wet slap as the boy's shattered skull cracked on to the pavement.

"Jerry!" I screamed, kneeling down in the wet road, cradling my friend in my arms, wondering madly how many times I'd seen the same scene in films, never expecting to live it out. He coughed as I pulled him closer, taking his pistol out of his hand and laying it down beside us. "Jerry, you fucking talk to me, man." His eyes, unblinking as the rain slowly fell into them, stared over to one side, seeing nothing except the rain diluting his own blood as it poured out of him and ran into the gutter. "Don't you fucking die!" I cried, hugging him without any response. "Don't die! It was just a kid, for fuck's sake!" He coughed again, small bubbles of blood running from the corner of his mouth. His arm spasmed and I kidded myself that he was trying to hold me, that it wasn't just his brain sending useless, crazy signals out as it shut itself down for good. I knelt in the rain and held my friend, crying as he bled, holding him until his short, ragged breaths stopped, then holding him some more.

Lights had come on in the street and dim silhouettes of people could be seen in one or two windows, probably woken by either the gunshot or my screams, or both. Off in the distance I could hear sirens, and marvelled at the fact that, despite the world's changes, some things were still the same: someone had called the cops.

I looked down at Jerry's face and stroked his lightly stubbled cheek. "Fuck," I whispered. Gently I laid him down on the road, then glanced around at the faces in the windows, watching them pull back slightly. The kid lay on the pavement, the top of his head open to the elements, and for a second I thought of trampling him, crushing his already broken skull and whatever remained inside for what he had done to my friend.

Instead, as the sirens grew louder, I ran off into the night, down the same alley the kid had appeared from, hoping that it wasn't a dead end.

I didn't think about Jerry's pistol, the one that I had pried from his fingers, until much later when I lay shivering beneath an angel in a graveyard.

Chapter Two

I woke to the raucous, righteous sound of church bells calling the faithful to do their Sunday duty. I was cold and wet, my back ached from the awkward position I had slept in and I was out of cigarettes. With great care I stood wincing as my back protested with indignant waves of pain. Leaning on the great granite base of the tombstone that I had sheltered next to, ignoring the sad look the angel above me cast in my direction, I glanced out into the open area in front of the church.

The vicar stood beneath the lich-gate, greeting the believers who nodded at him before making their way into the vast stone building; their shoulders hunched against the drizzle. One or two umbrellas surfaced, uniformly black as if the church wardens were giving them out as people arrived. The churchgoers seemed preocupied, sombre for the most part with thoughts of God and religion, though I thought a few faces bore the unmistakable signs of hangovers. Repent, ye sinners.

Ten years ago, the crowd that walked through the gate on it's way to prayer would have consisted almost entirely of middle-aged or older people: true believers brought up within the framework of Christianity that their parents and teachers had constructed for them and which had comforted them in their later years. Now the Sunday trip to church — whichever of the eight services a day you attended, at least one of which was mandatory — was a family affair. Grandfathers herded their extended families into the waiting bosom of Mother Church to be taught about the goodness and forgiveness of Christ. I wondered how they had taken the news of the Archbishop of Canterbury's murder yesterday, and how many sermons throughout the country today would be dealing with that very subject.

I sat back down behind the tombstone, my back complaining again like a dog that's been moved after he's made himself comfortable on the sofa. Wondering where I was going to go now, I patted my pockets for my fags, then remembered I'd smoked the last of them the night before. That brought back the memory of Jerry in my arms, his stomach bleeding out into the rain, his life draining away. I remembered taking his pistol out of his hand, and wondered if the Church Police or the RAF would get any fingerprints from it. It seemed fairly easy to deduce the fact that the kid had stabbed Jerry, but who had shot him in the head? If there were only Jerry's prints on the gun then there wouldn't be a problem, but I had handled it as well, however briefly. At the very least I was an accessory, and with the developments of the last few years, murder no longer carried a life imprisonment sentence. It didn't even carry a death sentence. Judging by the rumours, it was worse than that.

So I had to assume the Church Police, and probably the RAF, would want me "to help with their enquiries" which meant that they'd definitely have Jerry's place covered. They would have pulled my files and checked with any known friends in the area, so that probably ruled out Hal's place, even assuming he was still living at the same address he had been at the last time I visited him.

Sighing heavily and wishing for a cigarette, I reached into my denim jacket and pulled out Roller's business card. No address, just a phone number. I added a mobile phone to my wish list.

*

Nobody wears denim on a Sunday. Nobody wears anything other than their Sunday best, their church clothes. And nobody goes anywhere on a Sunday except to church, which made me stick out like a clown in a convent.

It took me almost an hour to find a phone box. I left the graveyard as quickly as I could, sneaking from one gravestone to another, hunched over in the grass that grew rich and green, fed as it was by the decaying flesh of the dead. At the rear of the church, the road was a bit lower than at the front and a drop of maybe ten feet caused a moment's worry. As it was, I lowered myself down, hanging until there were only a few feet or so between my boots and the ground, then I let go. Once I was down I found the nearest alley, planning to get off the main street and away from prying eyes as soon as I could.

The five years I'd spent away did me no favours as I

walked aimlessly through the back streets of London. Avoiding the main roads had seemed like a sensible idea, but now I was forced to wonder: how many phones were stuck off the beaten track? More than once I saw curtains twitch and figures move behind them, figures that would dart back into the safety of their darkened rooms when I turned to stare.

There was no music as I walked, no distant television or radio sounds; the only traffic that drifted along the roads held the faithful. The entire population of the country was at this moment either in church or on its way too or from there. No shops were open; if challenged as to why I was out and about dressed in normal clothing, I couldn't even fall back on saying I was off to the Asian corner shop to get some fags. Christian or not, no one opened on a Sunday anymore.

Finally, on one corner of a cross roads, a phone box sat waiting. I approached as nonchalantly as I could and slipped inside, fishing in my pockets for some change. Putting a fifty-pence piece in the phone, all the money I had, I took Roller's card out of my jacket, placed it on top of the phone and dialled the number. As the receiver purred contentedly into my ear, the cat that got the coin, I looked around at the houses. I wasn't surprised to find one or two curtains pulled aside, suspicious faces peering out at me. They were a braver breed of neighbour here, never flinching as I stared back at them.

The phone was picked up at the other end.

"Hello?" I asked after a moment's silence. My fifty credits began to diminish. A Sunday premium discouraged phone calls, one of the last liberties begrudgingly granted to the otherwise starved populace. "Roller?"

"Who is this?" A female voice.

"Aitch, Aitch McKean," I said without thinking. "I need to talk to Roller." There was silence from the other end and I pictured the woman checking with somebody. Already my credits were half gone.

"Where are you?" the woman asked suddenly. I looked around frantically, searching for a road sign or a distinctive shop. There seemed to be more people looking out of windows, and I thought one of them was on the phone himself, probably to the Church Police. Or the RAF.

"Russell Street," I said, catching sight of a street sign. "I'm at a phone box at a crossroads and one of the streets is Russell Street." I was babbling, panicking as I watched my credits vanish.

"Walk up Russell Street. Look for Turner Road. Walk down it." The woman hung up with only three credits left. Hooking the receiver back in place, and casting a nervous glance at the faces watching me, I quickly walked off, following her directions.

Things were worse walking away. As my tired feet carried me along the pavement, up Russell Street and into Turner Road, traffic slowly began to build. People began to return from church and at the same time, their neighbours were either getting ready to go or actually on their way to worship their God. Dark suits and pastel dresses became *de rigueur* around me as more and more people slipped from their cars or houses. All of them looked at me, dozens of eyes turned my way. Sooner or later, I thought, someone's going to say —

"Excuse me." It was a man, dark suit, white shirt, black tie. He could have been cast from the same mould as any of the other men around him. A woman, presumably his wife, stood on the other side of the car that he had just stepped from, her hand on the shoulder of a teenage boy who wore the same style of suit as his father. "Are you . . . from around here?" the man asked. I stared at him. I could see the few other people who had just come back from church hesitating near their cars and at their garden gates, watching us. Watching me.

"No." I said. "I'm not."

"I didn't think so." The man looked me up and down, taking in my denims, the jeans stained from kneeling in the rain with Jerry last night, the jacket grubby from sleeping in a graveyard. "I was just wondering if you were going to church. I could give you a lift, if you like."

"No, I'm not going to church."

He turned to his wife briefly. She nodded and steered the boy toward their house. Around me, I could see the scene being repeated along the street: dutiful wives and children going inside, indignant dark-suited men turning towards me.

"Would you like to tell us where you are going?" the man asked. The "us" became evident as he was joined by the other members of the faithful.

"Problem, Ed?" one of the newcomers asked.

"I was just asking this young man where he was off to if he wasn't going to church," Ed replied, smiling slightly.

"You not going to church, then, mate?" the second man asked, sneering at me.

A long black car pulled up beside us. One of the rear doors opened, and the tall, pale Upper who had been with Roller the night before stepped out. His eyes, hidden behind sunglasses, drifted across the crowd of men around me and one by one they all backed off. He looked at me and, without saying a word, indicated the car.

I smiled at Ed and his friends and climbed inside the dark interior. The Pale Man got in the front, closed the door and the driver pulled away.

*

Cars with dark windows were nothing new; I'd been in several police cars over the years. The outside surface of the glass appeared black to anyone looking in, while the driver and passengers saw through smoked windows.

The interior of this car was black. With all the doors closed I was blind. I felt the car drive off, steering effortlessly through the remainder of the traffic on the road, and I couldn't see a damn thing.

I gasped in surprise as the Pale Man switched on a small light set into the roof. He sat back, his round shades looking as if they'd been made from the same glass as the car's windows, and he smiled at nothing. The small bulb illuminated the driver, a fat coloured man whose grey suit jacket was stretched tight over his shoulders and whose poorly shaved head bulged from beneath the cap he wore; a stubbled roll of fat fell over his collar. He too had a pair of dark glasses on, ignoring the fact that the windows, despite the interior light, were still black.

Uppers were different from their darker counterparts. They were usually taller, and the one with tattoos was the first I'd seen with any sort of markings on his skin. There's less of them than the Downers, and it was strange to have seen one kind working with the other; most everyone assumed they were diametrically opposed, as contrary in their views and habits as they were in their appearance. With everything I'd seen over the years, I didn't know which group scared me the most.

*

When I met him again, Roller held court in much the same way that he had in the pub the previous night. But first I had to be taken before him. The Pale Man stepped out of the dark car with me when it stopped, before it drove off again and left us in a rubble-strewn warehouse courtyard. Puddles of filthy water, their surfaces decorated with oily rainbows, lay scattered across the yard like acne on a teenager's face, holes full of pustulence. A ruined car, its shell burnt and rusted in equal measure, lay like a drunkard against one wall of the large warehouse in front of us. The face of the building hung loosely as if the builders had thrown it together and almost missed; windows were smashed, guttering swung from the roof and rust grew like industrial ivy along the metal doors and frames.

The Pale Man grinned and again nodded, this time indicating the building. I hadn't heard him say a word, either today or last night, and I wondered whether he was a mute. I followed him into the warehouse, passing him when he held the corrugated door open for me. The inside was just as decrepit as the outside and stank of oil, cars, beer and the memory of illegal, years-old rave parties held in the dead of night.

In the gloom and the grime, Roller sat on a plush sofa that looked incongruous to say the least. Beside it, illuminating the scene, was a tall standard lamp, a fringed shade softening the light. Sat on the sofa with the big man was the pretty Oriental girl. Seeing her made the back of my neck itch, as if the burns the Downer had inflicted recognised her. The Pale Man left me standing in front of them and took his place at Roller's left hand.

"Mr McKean. What can I do for you?" Roller asked.

"I think I'm in trouble," I said, then told him about me and Jerry walking home the night before, about the stupid kid who had tried to mug us and what had happened after.

"So you handled the pistol?" Roller asked when I had finished.

"Yeah," I said, still surprised at my stupidity. "Jerry was dying, I wasn't thinking. It was raining, though. Hopefully the Church Police won't be able to lift my prints from it."

"They probably won't. The RAF, however . . . they are a different story."

The Religious Armed Forces were at the top of the law enforcement pyramid. Over the last ten years, since the world had been turned upside down, the Police had changed into the Church Police, but the RAF had been created to be the country's elite peace keeping force, and versions of this organization quickly spread throughout the world. The RAF's role quickly grew and changed until it became the top security force, investigating dissidents and activists, as well as any instance of the crime now deemed by the Godhead to be the most heinous: murder. The taking of a life, the breaking of the sixth Commandment was now rated as the single greatest crime in the country. And with the death of the young mugger, I was a party to it.

Roller looked up at me, his hand lightly stroking the Oriental girl's shoulder.

"The card I gave you with my number. May I have it?"

I smiled and reached into my pocket. Among the less legitimate members of society, it was standard practice to keep links between a murder suspect and yourself down to the barest minimum. The last thing Roller wanted was for me to get picked up and have the RAF find a card . . .

I didn't have it. As my fingers fished around in my pockets trying to conjure the small piece of paper, my smile faded. Roller's expression quickly matched my own, a look of dismayed surprise. "You don't have it? Did you phone me from memory?" he asked. I remembered reading the number as I dialled it, looking at the card as it sat on top of the payphone.

"Oh shit," I whispered. I let my wandering hand fall

limp at my side and shrugged. "I don't have it," I said.

"Did you leave it in the phone box?" Roller asked. I nodded. He sighed, his big barrel chest rising and falling as he closed his eyes, his nostrils flaring gently, giving the impression of someone struggling to hold on to his temper. "Charlotte," he said. The Oriental girl dipped into a small bag that she held and withdrew a mobile phone. She stood up as she dialled a number, then walked behind the sofa towards the rear of the warehouse as she talked. Roller slowly looked at me, leaning forward in his seat, his elbows resting on his knees, his hands held tightly together. "I offered you my help last night. It was only through the intervention of my colleague that the Downers did not carry you off. I gave you my card so that, if you needed to, you could ring me. It was also a form of contract. By accepting it, you also took responsibility for it and thus responsibility to me. By your act of negligence, you have betrayed that trust."

"It's only a card," I said. He had mentioned none of this responsibility crap to me the night before, and I was damned if he was going to land it on me now.

"A card bearing a number which could be traced to me. A number which was dialled by someone from a phone box on a Sunday, someone who was obviously not dressed for church. Someone, furthermore, who is almost certainly under investigation by at the very least the police, if not the damned RAF. It was more than just a card, McKean!"

I put my hands up as he stood and stormed over to me, the Pale Man following quickly behind him, a grin on his face. Despite my beating the mugger the previous night, I'm not much good in a fight. If I can get in quick and hard I've got a chance, but with Roller thundering toward me, I saw only one option and took it.

I darted left, my DMs splashing through a few puddles the worn-out roof had let in, and crashed through the corrugated door, out into the courtyard. I heard Roller scream "GET HIM!" and somehow found time to grin at his lack of originality. Once out of the building I had no idea where I was; I had travelled here blind. So, running on pure instinct, I again dodged left, remembering too late that the car had driven off in that direction. Behind me came the soft padding steps of the Pale Man. I wasn't going to waste time looking back over my shoulder at him.

I reached the corner of the building, but instead of diving around it, I carried on into a place that was either a disused car lot or an automobile graveyard. Cars of every sort, piled two or three high in places, squatted on their wheel rims or rotted tyres, their windows smashed or removed, their wiring and panelling hanging off at crazy angles like a schoolboy's hair in the morning. Without thinking, I moved from one aisle to another, taking turns left and right as I saw them, moving further and further into the auto mortuary. Finally, my cigarette-racked lungs screaming at me, I slowed to a walk, then stumbled to a stop. I rested against two cars, the upper having crushed the roof of the lower flat. Gasping frantically for breath, swearing I was going to quit smoking yet dying for a fag, I looked back the way I had come, expecting to see the Pale Man.

He wasn't there. I'd lost him. Trouble was, I'd lost myself too. Pushing myself away from the cars, I trudged my way along the oil-stained and glass-littered aisles, looking for a way out, wondering where I was going to go.

Chapter Three

There's nowhere to hide on a Sunday. You can't go out, except to church, unless you're a gangster with your own warehouse tucked away in the middle of nowhere. If you're a tired bloke with what feels like the entire world after you, things are a little tougher.

Once I had my breath back, I made my way as quickly and as quietly as I could out of the wrecked car lot, in a direction which I hoped was away from Roller's warehouse. Climbing over a wooden fence, I landed in a scrubby wilderness: bare patches of earth vied with clumps of dry brown grass; stones and rocks, as well as broken bottles and tin cans, littered the desolate landscape. The ground rolled and dipped in small hills and hollows and a few miles away, looking grey and uninviting in the cloud-smeared mid-morning sun, was the edge of the city. At the very least I had a rough idea of where I was: outside London. This far out, and especially in this place, the chances of being spotted by anyone were practically nil; even the Church Police and the RAF had Sundays off with the exception of attendance patrols.

Slowly, it began to rain. I looked up at the sky and squinted against the few droplets that spattered against my face, figuring this was just typical. As I walked off, heading down one of the rubble mounds and into the meandering paths between them, I buttoned up my denim and hunched my shoulders. The rain brought back the memory of Jerry from the night before, how he'd been stabbed and died in my arms. How had everything become so shitty in such a short time?

Whether it was fate, luck, or God I don't know, but something threw me a small break then. Rounding one of the mounds of concrete and dirt, my feet splashing through the grimy rain water collecting around them, I saw a ramshackle attempt at a hut. Made from FOR SALE hoardings and other odds and ends, it looked to be cut into the side of one of the mounds. Head down, I ran for it.

The inside wasn't brilliant: it went into the mound for only a couple of feet, but it was wide enough to house two plastic chairs, both of which were covered in ragged black and white strips, the skins of carrier bags hunted down in the wilderness. Slumping on to one of the chairs, I unbuttoned my jacket, brushed my wet hair off my face and wished to God I had some cigarettes. At least this place was dry and out of the wind. Looking around, it didn't give the impression of being anything more than a place to wait out the rain; there was no way it could have been lived in full time. Apart from the chairs there was no other furniture, and a few rusted cans at the back of the place were the only evidence that any meals had been eaten here. Whoever had made this place had either moved on for good or hadn't been here for a long time.

"Get the fuck out of there."

I looked out into the rain. A young woman stood looking in at me, her wide-brimmed black hat dripping rain down on to her long greatcoat, the collar of which she held closed with her gloved left hand. She looked too thin and pale to be healthy, and she didn't look pleased to see me. In her right hand, held down at her side, she gripped the handle of a machete, the big, broad blade polished and lethal.

Slowly, I raised my hands up. "Hey, I was only getting out of — "

"Get the fuck out of there," she repeated, this time levelling the blade at me. I shut up and got to my feet, edging slowly out of the shelter and back into the rain, the pair of us staring at each other. Considering the way she looked, it was possible I could have grabbed the machete off her before she had a chance to use it, but over the last couple of days I'd seen one too many blades used to feel comfortable with taking that chance. The woman edged backwards into the shelter and sat in the chair I'd used. With her free hand, she pushed the other chair out towards me. "Sit down," she commanded. For a second I felt like telling her to piss off, but with all the hassle I'd had, I just slumped into the chair, crossed my arms and stared back at her. "What do you want with me?" she asked.

"Lady, the only things I want right now are to be dry and have a fag. The only reason I was in that hut of yours was like I said: I was just getting out of the rain. I don't know who you are, and to be honest I'm not all that interested." Actually, this last was a lie. I wanted to know why she was out here and what the hell she was doing living on a piece of brownfield land.

She thrust the knife into the ground at her side with a soft *shunk* and pushed her chair further back. "Okay, get in here." I didn't need her to ask twice, and a second later we were both huddled under the hoardings. "What's your name?" she asked.

"Aitch McKean," I said, holding out my hand. Her own tiny hand was enveloped in mine, but there was strength in those slim bones when she squeezed.

"Aitch?"

"Yeah, Aitch. Like the letter. It stands for something, but don't ask what." She shrugged and pulled her coat tighter around herself. "What about you?"

She took her hat off and ruffled her short, spiky hair before raising her dark eyes to me. "Rhea," she said with a shrug. "So you didn't come out here looking for me?" she asked, her hand dropping subtly towards the machete.

"Tell you the truth, Rhea, I don't know where the hell I am. I got into a spot of bother, did a runner and ended up in this place. It started to rain, I saw this hut so I thought I'd wait out the storm." I glanced out through the wide-open entrance. "Which looks as if it's getting worse." I turned back to her and asked, as casually as I could, "Why would anyone be looking for you?"

She shrugged again, settling back in her chair, pouting slightly. She seemed to think for a moment before making a decision. Reaching inside her coat, she brought out a packet of cigarettes and a box of matches, smiling gently at my eager gaze. Rhea handed one over to me, took one for herself, then leaned forward and lit them both from the same match. Sitting back, breathing out her fragrant blue smoke, she watched me for a few seconds.

"I've been known to do some work for . . . various people," she said. "Some of them know how to get in touch with me. I thought you might be from them."

"What sort of work is it you do?"

"What sort of trouble are you in?" she countered.

I thought for a moment, glancing out at the crap weather beyond our cast-off hideaway. "My friend got killed last night. Some kid tried to mug us. He stabbed my friend, then my friend shot him. I may have handled the gun, which means the RAF will probably want to have a word with me. There's also a gangster involved, plus I had a run-in with a couple of Downers."

"Downers?" Rhea said. "Mr McKean, it sounds like you had a busy night. Who were you running from to get here?"

"The gangster. I may have accidentally mixed him up in Jerry's death last night. Needless to say, he wasn't too happy. Tried to get one of his guys to give me a working over, but I managed to slip past him." I shrugged. "Ended up in here. Your turn."

Rhea smiled and flicked her ash from her cigarette, brushing it off her coat when the wind blew it back at her.

"I do lots of stuff for the right price," she said.

"Are you a prostitute?" I asked before wincing at my clumsy stupidity.

"Why? You desperate for a fuck as well as a fag?" She chuckled when I blushed. "No, Mr McKean, I'm not," she said with an indulgent smile. "I help certain groups to obtain or release various objects or persons. Any more than that, it's probably best you don't know."

"A woman of mystery, eh?"

"No, a woman who takes precautions. What are you going to do now?"

I looked back out of the hut, at the grey wall which surrounded London.

"Wait until dark, or until it stops raining, then try and get back into the city. It'll be tough, what with it being Sunday and all, but I think I can manage."

"How long has it been since you had to get back in after curfew?" Rhea asked with a smile.

"A few years," I admitted. I had the feeling that Rhea

29

might not be the weak woman with a big knife I'd originally taken her to be, and if she could help me get back into the city, I'd be more than obliged. I asked if she could help.

"Sure, but why do you want to go back? The RAF are probably after you, you've got gangsters and Downers on your case as well. Why the hell go back?"

It was my turn to smile. "I have my reasons," I said. "You're not the only one with secrets,"

*

It came as no surprise that Rhea agreed to help me for a small fee, one which I could pay her when we returned, plus I think she was just plain curious. She spent the remaining hours of the day filling me in on what had happened in the country during the five years I'd been away, though I'd heard some of it while I was abroad.

What had started off as a resurgence in Christian thought had turned into a virtual political movement, its popularity increased a thousandfold when the self-proclaimed Godhead appeared. Britain, still racked by the troubles that had swallowed the country whole after the turn of the century, was crying out for anything other than another round of the same politicians who had plunged the place into chaos. The Godhead was seen as the answer to the nation's prayers and quickly, under his guidance, the country had become a theocracy, managed first by the Church Police, and later by the RAF. Laws were enforced to make church attendance at least twice a week mandatory. People of other religions were at first tolerated, though in later years their presence was less and less welcome; there was talk of camps and pogroms, but nothing had ever been proven.

With the advent of first the Uppers and then the Downers, the power balance had begun to shift slightly as more and more of them worked their way into a variety of roles, either independently or for groups other than the official ruling class. The Godhead, the first of the Uppers to appear, tried to get every new upper working with him, and to discourage any true believers' involvement with the Downers. As the number of Uppers and Downers increased, though, their involvement in day-to-day situations became impossible to regulate. The Uppers were a lot more human looking and found it easier to become part of society; it helped that the country's spiritual leader was one of them. The Downers, shunned in large by the respectable people, seemed to gravitate toward the more disreputable end of the market.

London was the Godhead's stronghold. It seemed to have taken him ten minutes to rise to power, willingly aided and abetted by a general public tired of sleazy politicians and desperate for something new, something spiritual. Appealing to jingoistic nationalism didn't hurt him, either. But nowadays he didn't appear in public much anymore, leaving the bureaucracy to his "elected" officials.

"Of course," Rhea said, "once Britain had elected an Upper to govern them, whether or not the voting was rigged, it paved the way for other countries. Most of Europe now has an Upper as head of state, and while the American president is still normal, his two closest advisers are both Uppers. The Godhead here has no real competition and can do pretty much what he wants." She sighed. "And that's how things're gonna be unless someone changes it."

We'd smoked the last of her cigarettes by the time dusk settled over the rubble. Slowly, we readied ourselves to go back into London, even though the border patrol and curfew guards would be out.

"How are we going to get into the city, then?" I asked. Rhea smiled at me, put her hat on and clicked the machete on to a magnetic scabbard strapped to her thigh. "Can we bypass the wall?"

Rhea shook her head. "Not unless you want to go miles out of your way. It's pretty much finished round these parts. But don't worry, we'll get in. All you have to do is *what* I tell you, *when* I tell you and to remain quiet. One word could completely bugger us up. Agreed?"

I nodded, doing my jacket back up against the cold wind of evening. At least it had stopped raining.

*

There's a wall most of the way round London, twenty

feet tall and at least as thick. Every fifty feet or so squats a sentry tower, always manned with armed guards. Searchlights perch on top of the towers, their blank, bright gaze trained out on the surrounding countryside and on the roads that stab into the wall like swords in an old-fashioned magician's basket. Opinion is divided as to whether the wall is there to keep people out or keep them in. Patrolling along the wall, their own powerful torches and weapons ever ready, are members of the Church Police, vigilantly watching the travellers going back and forth throughout the week, checking travel passes and reasons for leaving and entering.

With sunset almost upon us, the entire city rang with the sound of church bells calling the faithful. Hundreds, perhaps thousands of God's houses, each equipped with from four to twenty bells, shouted out their invitations and exhortations, deafening believers and sinners alike.

Rhea and I left the rubble mounds behind us and crossed over scrubland, where grasses grew wild and unkempt amongst the remains of what looked to be an old rail junction. Dark patches on the ground, bereft of any but the hardiest vegetation, spoke of oil leaks and engine grease, summoning images of an earlier time. My father had worked on the railways; that was all I really knew of him.

My parents, a railway man and a lonely woman made old before her time by crushing poverty and a string of diseased lovers, left each other and me in the same week. I was four years old when my mother didn't come back from going down the shops. She phoned my father later in the evening, and while I can't remember the actual conversation, I can picture him standing in the hall, the phone to his ear. He shrugged, his orange safety jacket, a bright day-glo nightmare, jerking up stiffly, the material coarse and hard. He put the phone down, looked over at me — the snot- and food-stained fruit of his loins — and left the house.

It must have been almost a week before I was discovered by a burglar who, in the process of rifling the house for something she could sell, found me sitting happily eating the last of the packet cereal I'd opened and staring fixedly at the television. She smiled at me when she had my attention and picked me up, holding me up to the light and cooing nonsense, chuckling when I laughed back at her.

She sold me to a Child Catcher, one of a breed of men that had grown out of the need for parents to rid themselves of their children after the troubles, when childless people were receiving better benefits than those with kids. A modern-day Fagin, Ymir Qizilbash — a name which I didn't learn to spell until I was about thirteen — was fortunately one of the better of his kind. He taught me to read and write, and schooled me in other basic skills such as maths, cooking meals from nothing, pick pocketing and, on occasion when I was older, the finer art of assault and battery, not that I was much good at that. It was at the "Qizilbash Orphanage" that I met Hal.

"Hey," Rhea said, bursting into my reverie. "You still with me?" As I'd let my mind wander thinking about things I hadn't bothered with for years, I'd lagged behind her. I muttered an apology and jogged over to where she knelt behind some rusted hulk that may once have been a rail carriage.

"What now?" I asked her.

"We wait," she said, looking at me as if I was stupid. At that moment I felt it.

"For what?"

"Aitch, it's Sunday. How much traffic goes in or out of the city on a Sunday?" When she saw that I understood, she sat down, pulling her coat tight around her frame. "We can't get in until at least midnight, if not a bit later. We may as well get some rest."

I slumped down beside her, fragments of rust coating my jacket and falling down the back of my neck, irritating the scabbed-over scorch marks.

"So why do you need to get back in, anyway?" Rhea asked eventually. I ran my hand over my stomach, wincing slightly.

"To get some food for a start. I'm fucking starving." The last thing I'd eaten had been some home-made chili Jerry had cooked up before we went out to the pub. Realising I hadn't eaten for twenty-four hours did my stomach no good at all.

"No, seriously."

"I told you earlier: we all have our secrets. Mine just happens to be in there." I poked my thumb in the direction of the far-off wall.

"Whereabouts?" she asked. "If I'm going to get you in, I need to know where we're going,"

I sighed, loathe to give out any information, but knowing she had a right to it. "You know Whitechapel?" She nodded. "One of the roads round there, Nichols Row."

"What's there?"

"Jerry's house. My mate who was killed last night. Chances are the RAF have been and gone. They might have left a copper there, but I doubt it. I need to get something from his place."

"What?"

I chuckled at her persistence. "I told you, it's a secret."

"Okay," Rhea said. "As long as I get my cash for getting you back in."

We fell quiet then as the last of the sun disappeared, the clouds above the city glowing a pale orange from the street lamps and church lights, blocking out the stars. As soon as midnight arrived, I was planning to put my trust in a woman whom I'd only just met, and expect her to get me back into the city.

Convinced I was crazy, I closed my eyes and tried to sleep.

Chapter Four

Rhea woke me with a shake; darkness greeted me and I had to blink twice before I was convinced that my eyes were open. Without a word, she led me off to the left, towards the embankment leading up to the road into the city. We stumbled through the litter-strewn grass, or rather I did; Rhea seemed to float above the ground without making a sound, and only looked back at me to scowl through the ill-lit night when a can I'd kicked rattled across the dirt before coming to a stop. Perhaps half an hour later (it was difficult to judge the time) we reached the bottom of the bank and, following Rhea's lead, I knelt down.

"What now?" I whispered after a moment, more to break the silence than for any other reason. She fumbled in the pocket of her long coat and brought something out that fitted into the palm of her hand.

"We need to get up to the top of the bank, that much should be obvious. Stay below the top of it, and get ready to move when I say so. We need to find a car that'll suit us."

I nodded, not really understanding what she meant. We commando-crawled up the bank, shale and stone digging into my knees and elbows, and I marvelled that I'd never felt any discomfort when I'd done this as a child, playing soldiers with Hal and the other kids from Qizilbash's. Maybe kids were made of tougher stuff?

Rhea inched her way a little further than me, her hat just cresting the level of the road, peeping through the steel guard fence away from the city, in the direction of approaching traffic. I saw that what she was holding was a pair of binoculars, small and black.

"How can you see?" I whispered. She looked back at me, then handed them across. As I looked through the lenses, the night instantly became green, as if someone had slipped me some acid and sent me on an environmentally friendly trip. The black cross-hairs in the centre of each night-sight lens detracted from the sensation, though. I handed the binoculars back, and Rhea went back to her vigil, scanning the infrequent cars.

I drifted, sleep lulling me back into its arms, taunting me with the promise of comforting dreams. "Aitch, get up here," Rhea said suddenly, standing up and vaulting over the fence. I scrabbled up on to the top and slowly climbed over. "Get on the floor as if you've been knocked over," she said, stuffing her binoculars back into her coat and pulling her hat over her face slightly. "Don't say a word or do anything until I tell you."

"You think this is gonna work?" I asked.

"Oldest trick in the book. One of them, anyway. Now shut up and do as I say."

I wasn't sure I had any choice. In a fit of amateur dramatics, I collapsed on to the hard tarmac, cracking my head loudly on one of the cat's eyes for my troubles. "Shit!" I hissed, only to be silenced by Rhea's army boot in my thigh. She knelt at my head, cradling me in her lap, not out of tenderness, I realised, but rather to complete the tableau of the injured and the comforter. "Keep quiet," she hissed. I closed my eyes, adrenaline making sure I wasn't going to fall asleep again.

A car slowly came to a stop a few feet away, its headlights capturing our little drama. A door opened and a man's voice asked if we were all right.

"We've been . . . robbed," Rhea sobbed quietly. "My husband . . . they beat him up . . . stole our car." This is never going to work, I thought, and sure enough, the car door *thunked* shut. I almost stood then, but Rhea's hand kept me still and a second later there was the sound of shoes crunching over gravel as the driver walked over to us.

"How badly hurt is he?" he asked. The headlights were dimmed slightly, and I imagined him leaning over, hands on his knees, trying to spot an injury.

"It's his leg, I think," Rhea said in her best lost-housewife voice. There was a pause then, for only a couple of seconds, as the driver looked at her, taking in her clothes. My head cracked back on to the road as she suddenly moved, her machete sliding free of its magnetic sheath with a quiet *shing!* before embedding itself in the man's neck. I looked up to see her push him back to the fence and kick him over, pulling her blade free with the same movement. By the time I sat up, there was nothing to indicate the man had ever been there, except for his car and one or two small splashes of blood that dripped from Rhea's machete. She sniffed and spat on the road before pulling on a pair of gloves.

"You got any?" she asked, holding hers up as she covered her hands.

"No," I said, looking over at the fence. "You killed him."

"Of course I did. Nobody *walks* down this road — there's no pavement, see? — and if he'd reached the city he would have reported us and the car. This way at least he won't be missed for a day or two." She chuckled. "Unless of course that was one of the Godhead's ministers, but I doubt it." Rhea moved around to the rear of the car and tried opening the boot. It was locked. She grabbed the keys from the ignition, killing the lights and the engine, then opened it up as I joined her. With a small pencil light held in her mouth, taken from another of her pockets, we scanned the two leather suitcases and their contents: clothes and the odds and ends of a weekend out of the city, nothing more exciting than that. As I reached for something, she slapped my hand away.

"Don't touch anything. When you get in the car put your hands in your lap, or better still your jacket pockets, and keep them there. The last thing you want is for your prints to be discovered in the car of a man who will be found dead at some point." She thumped the boot shut, then opened my door for me, closing it after I was in. "Pretend to be asleep. If the guards at the wall need to ask you something, our story is that we're a brother and sister visiting our parents. They may have seen the car stop; if so we had a slight problem with the engine. The fan belt's always a good one. Once we fixed it, we were on our way again."

As she pulled away and headed for the city, I found myself wondering just how many times she'd done this before. And I wondered how many more people would die because of me.

*

Through half-shut eyes I watched the city's approach, the spotlight-illuminated crossing point getting nearer and nearer, growing steadily in the dirt-smeared windscreen. It reminded me of the old Mexican border crossings I'd seen in movies, or toll booths on a bridge. The four lanes of approaching traffic, though there was only ourselves and one other car by the time we arrived, split so that each lane was fed between sentry boxes. There were two guards at each armed with what appeared to be to my uneducated eyes, big fuck-off rifles. These were Church Police, distinguished by their matte black uniforms and white Maltese cross insignia and entrusted with preventing undesirables entering the city or criminals escaping. Rhea was hoping that, at a quarter to one in the morning, they weren't being too picky.

A guard waved us forward up to the barrier and motioned that Rhea should unwind her window, while his partner watched us both, his rifle poised in his arms, cradled like a baby.

"That your car that stopped back there?" he asked, his breath frosting in through the window. Rhea came up with the simple story of a loose fan belt which she'd managed to fix. The guard grunted. "Who's your friend?" he said. I had slumped against the window and now, with his attention focused on me, did my best impression of a slumbering idiot, my mouth slightly open as I breathed slowly and deeply.

"My brother. You want me to wake him?"

"Nah, I suppose not," the guard said. "How comes you're entering the city this early in the morning?"

"We've both got jobs to go to tomorrow, or today rather, and I didn't fancy the long queues in the day time." The guard grunted again and I clearly heard him move his rifle. Was he pointing it at us?

A moment later Rhea started the car up again, and slowly drove off. With the lack of cold air, I assumed she'd wound the window up.

"Don't say anything, or move a muscle," she said. "They could still be watching us." She drove slowly through the dead streets of the city and I had almost dozed off for real by the time she sighed and said I could move.

"You could have let me sleep," I whined, sitting up and knuckling my eyes. I'd woken up far too early that morning, I'd had a crap day and I could have done with a good few hours' sleep.

"And how would I get to your mate's house?"

I rearranged myself on the leather seat before placing my hands back in my jacket, then gave Rhea directions to Jerry's house.

The streets were incredibly quiet. We saw only three other vehicles, and two of those were old-fashioned milk floats, resurrected because of their quiet electric engines which didn't disturb the post-Sunday peace too much. Shops and office buildings, public and private houses — all were in darkness, as if everyone except us had died and was in mourning.

The drive from the gate to Whitechapel took perhaps an hour, and was made infinitely easier by the lack of other traffic. As we approached Jerry's road, Rhea pulled the car in and stepped out, walking around to the other side to let me out as well. "If there's anyone awake around here — "

"Yeah, I can guess. Leave the car a couple of streets away so that nobody sees it pull up outside Jerry's," I whispered. "I'm not exactly a virgin at this sort of thing." I walked off into the darkness, grinning at having guessed what Rhea had been about to say, and more than a little annoyed at her ease in handling the situation up to this point. She followed behind me as we walked the few hundred yards round to Nichols Row. We both paused on the corner, hiding behind the wall of the end house. I pointed out Jerry's place and Rhea scanned it with her binoculars, then checked out the surrounding area.

"It looks clear," she whispered.

I reached into my jeans pocket and pulled out the spare door key that Jerry had given me while I was staying there. Taking a deep breath, we walked quickly across the road, up the three small steps that led to Jerry's door, unlocked it and were inside.

"No lights," Rhea whispered. Her coat rustled and once

again she looked through the binoculars, checking the hallway. "Shit. It's full of junk. We'd make too much noise in the dark."

"I could have told you that," I said and reached for the light switch. "Careful of your eyes." The blinding flash of the light bulb pierced deep into my head even though I had my hand covering my eyes. Painfully slowly, squinting and blinking like a hedgehog dragged out from its bush at noon, I looked around at the garishly papered hallway, filled with black bags and a rucksack. "This junk, as you call it, happens to be my belongings."

"Great," Rhea said. "Find what you came for and let's get out of here."

I stepped through the hall, tiptoeing past my gear, and headed for the kitchen. "In a second," I call-whispered back to her. "I'm fucking starving."

"Aitch, we haven't got time," she said, following me. With the kitchen light on, I began raiding Jerry's well-stocked fridge, picking out bits and pieces with which to make a couple of sandwiches.

"I'll be five seconds," I placed bread, margarine, chicken, ham and cheese on the counter and looked around for a butter knife, finding one in the sink. Rhea watched as I put together a slap-dash chicken sandwich, biting into it even as I began the next.

"Is it me or is it warm in here?"

I shrugged. "Jerry must have left the heating on," I said. A second later, I looked up at her, then over her shoulder. She turned and stared.

A Downer stood in the doorway, his big white grin splitting the charcoal of his skin, droplets of red (blood, lava or whatever the hell it was) trickling down his face. His suit, black with the usual white shirt and black tie, smouldered gently. His eyes, dark pits with a burning flame deep inside, stared past Rhea and looked directly at me.

"Mr McKean. Would you come with me, please? My superiors would like a word with you."

Without taking my gaze off him, I spat the mouthful of

sandwich out into the sink. Rhea moved back towards me, staring at the Downer.

"About what?"

"Your little indiscretion last night. Plus your friend who appears to have a . . . certain special someone working for him."

"I don't know who you're talking about," I said, wishing I had something more than a butter knife to defend myself.

"Oh, I think you do." The Downer stepped forward; a wave of hot air rolled towards us, bringing sweat out on my brow. "Your somewhat clichéd gangster friend and the remarkable Upper who works for him."

"The Pale Man?" I asked. He was obviously who the Downer was on about, but I didn't know what made him so remarkable; all he'd done was stand up to the Tattooed Man.

"That's the one." The Downer placed his hand on the counter, near my sandwich, as we stepped back, coming to a halt against the cupboards. The cheap Formica on the surface bubbled beneath his skin, while the corners of my sandwich began to toast slightly.

"Hey, listen," Rhea said, "I don't want any of this, okay? I'm just going to move out the way; you can take him and I'll leave. All right?"

I stared at her, mute, watching her step away from me, off to one side. The Downer didn't even look at her. He stepped forward, his grin widening as he reached out to take hold of my jacket. There was a *shing!* as Rhea grabbed me and pulled me to her, in the same motion slicing her machete through the Downer's arm. His forearm erupted forward, propelled by the release of internal pressure, crashing into the wall, burying itself wrist deep. He screamed and fell to his knees, clutching at the molten mess that now poured out of his elbow, searing lumps of red-hot liquid that burst like wax bubbles only to solidify momentarily before bursting anew, over and over again. As the stuff hit the floor tiles, it ignited faintly, eating through the floor, creating potholes around him.

"Go!" Rhea shouted, pushing me over the counter, following me through the door and back into the hall, the banshee wails of the Downer echoing after us, pursuing us in gusts of hot air. We were through the main door before I quickly doubled back. "Aitch!"

I reappeared a moment later with my rucksack.

We bolted down the street, heedless of the few lights that were appearing in the windows around us.

A car blocked our escape, screeching to a halt ahead of us. The passenger door at the back opened.

"Aitch, get in!" Hal's pink topknot glowed almost fluorescent as he looked at me, beckoning madly. I wondered, for a moment, if Roller had sent him then Rhea pulled me in. Hal put his foot down, and we were gone.

Chapter Five

"Why should I trust you, Hal?" I asked him around a mouthful of bacon sandwich.

It was about 4 o'clock on Monday afternoon. Last night, he'd driven us through the back streets of the city, avoiding the increasing number of districts that were monitored by CCC-TV, the church-owned, RAF-run security system. By the time we reached Hal's place we were exhausted, the day's adventures catching up with us. Rhea crashed out in the spare room, I had the sofa and we slept for most of the day.

Now, after a shower and a change of clothes, I sat with my old friend, wondering whether he was going to sell me out. The shower steamed down the hall as Rhea washed.

"You should trust me because I'm your friend, Aitch."

"You also work for Roller, a man who is not very happy with me at the moment."

Hal smiled, taking a sip of his tea. "Yeah, I heard. Sounds like you fucked up, mate." He looked at me as seriously as he could with a pink top knot waving ludicrously above his dark features. "But I'm not going to turn you in to him." He sat back in his chair, pushing his empty plate away from him on the floor. "He asked me about you yesterday, don't get me wrong. I told him Saturday was the first time I'd seen you for five years, and that I'd only met your mate Jerry a couple of times before. I didn't know where the fuck you were, and that was the truth at the time. What I didn't tell him was that I knew where Jerry lived. A friend of a friend knew that little titbit as she'd bought some gear off him a while back."

"What sort of gear?"

"Doesn't matter. I hung around Jerry's house after I heard about yesterday, and while I didn't see you go in, I caught you coming out in a big hurry. What happened in there?"

I told him briefly about trying to grab some food and my stuff and about the Downer who had been waiting for us. Hal smiled when I mentioned Rhea and her machete.

"That me you're talking about?" she said, as she walked into the room still towelling her hair. It was the first time I'd seen her without her long coat and hat on. Her hair was longer at the back than I'd first thought, and as she ruffled it dry, the top spiked up no matter how much she smoothed it down. She was thin, her jeans and T-shirt baggy over her small frame, her hips and nipples poking out through the material. Grabbing a piece of my sandwich, she slumped into one of the seats.

"Yeah. Aitch was just telling me how you dealt with that Downer," Hal said. Rhea shrugged.

"An old trick. Those bastards get their mind set on one thing and it's fairly easy to surprise them." She looked over at me. "Well, I got you into the city again. Now I need my payment."

"Aren't you going to stick around? I could do with your help," I said.

"No, you can get yourself another sidekick, maybe Hal here. Me, I work on my own. You asked me to get you in, which I did, now I want to get paid. Simple arrangement." She wolfed down the last of my sandwich, then flung the towel over the back of her chair.

I sighed, genuinely disappointed that she was leaving. I'd hoped that she'd be along for the ride, even though she could have no idea of where that ride was going to go. Standing, I retrieved my rucksack from the other side of the room. I placed it between my legs as I sat down again, rummaging though the clothes and odds and ends until I found a thick A4 envelope.

"Christ, Aitch," Hal said as I reached in and took out a wad of notes, peeled some off and handed them to Rhea. Nowhere near as crass as Hal, she folded them up and slipped them into her jeans pocket.

"You need a hand again, Aitch, you know where to find me."

"That's just it Rhea. I will need a hand."

"What are you mixed up in, Aitch? What's in that rucksack that made you come back for it?" Hal asked.

I chuckled. "Just something I need for a bit later on."

"Oh come on, Aitch," Hal said. "You've got the Church Police and the RAF after you; you've got Downers fucking staking out houses trying to get you; you've even got Roller and his pet bloody Upper mad at you. It's got to be more than just a load of cash."

"Yeah, it is, but it's better you don't know. Senseless getting involved."

"Fuck off, mate; I *am* involved. I'm the one who got you away from that house last night. I'm fucking in this up to me neck, ain't I?" He paused, toying with the rings on his fingers. "You don't make it easy, do you?"

I thought for a second about what he'd said. "So what's the deal with that Upper working for Roller? The pale one with the shades?"

"That pale fucker, my friend, is Roller's new right-hand man even though he's not really a man, is he?" I looked at him strangely. "Well, come on, would you call Downers human? Course you wouldn't. Neither are Uppers."

"How much do you know much about them, Hal? Where they come from?"

"Which ones, Uppers or Downers?"

"Both."

"Where are they from?" He shrugged. "Where do you think?" He sat forward in his seat. "You know more and more of them have appeared over the last few years, yeah? Well, there's a rumour going round that says every time someone dies, another Downer or another Upper appears in the world. Now then, where do people go when they die?"

"Are you talking about Heaven and Hell?" I smiled at him.

"Don't laugh, Aitch. Since the Godhead appeared there have been no births. None. Anywhere. Did you know that? Nobody has been born for years, and no one knows why, but people are still dying, and every time one of those people dies, another Upper or Downer appears." His eyes began to gleam as he talked faster, his hands waving in front of him.

"Heaven and Hell are full up! There's nowhere for the dead people to go unless they push someone out who's already there. That's why there's more Downers than Uppers; more people go to Hell, so more Downers are sent back here with

their burnt skin and hot blood and stuff. But some people go to
Heaven. They're the ones who force the Uppers to come back
and if anything, the Uppers are much worse than the Downers.
See, the Downers, they've been stuck in Hell for fuck knows
how long. Coming back here's got to be like a holiday, but the
Uppers . . . they have to leave Paradise. They're extremely
fucking pissed off. Downers you can mess around with; Uppers you daren't touch. The one that Roller's got working
with him, he's only been around a couple of months but he
knows how to handle himself."

"How do you know?" I asked.

"Saturday night in the pub? That tattooed Upper with
the Downer? He should have walked off with you, but the pale
guy stopped him, yeah?"

"I remember," I said, thinking back to the Tattooed
Upper's eyes and the feeling of almost being hypnotised.

"The Pale Man just shook his head and wagged his finger. The Tattooed Man could tell he was out of his depth. For
one Upper to do that to another he's got to be powerful."

Rhea spoke up. "So Uppers and Downers are Angels
and Demons?"

"No, no, no," Hal said shaking his head. "They're dead
people who've been forced out of Heaven or Hell, and sooner
or later the world will be full of nothing else but them." We
looked at him, waiting for him to continue. "There have been
no births," he repeated. "Because of that, there's a finite number of people on this planet, all of whom are gonna die eventually, and all of them will be replaced by an Upper or a Downer.
Ten, twenty, maybe thirty years down the line, there's going to
be a war between them. Uppers against Downers. Sure, they
work together now, perhaps, but that's gonna change. They're
going to go to war, and the winners will have the Earth.

"Why do you think the Godhead amalgamated all the
churches? Enforced worship? So that when people die they'll
go to Heaven and create more Uppers. Why do you think
murder is the number-one sin? Because if someone kills someone who doesn't believe yet, they'll create another Downer.
Why do you think the Godhead killed the Archbishop of Can-

terbury? Not just because he spoke out against the Godhead's programme of combining religions. I mean, the Archbishop may be dead but you can bet he released another Upper into the world."

Rhea and I sat stunned as Hal finished his outburst. He knew, or thought he did, what was happening in the world. Some of what he said was right — I knew that — but the part about Heaven and Hell, the black and white theological part . . . even knowing what I did, I still found it difficult to accept.

Rhea turned to me. "Time for me to go," she said, raising her eyebrows at Hal's speech.

"Wait," I said as she stood. "Like I said, I'm going to need help. How about I pay you a retainer, a daily fee? A hundred quid a day?"

Rhea raised an eyebrow. "For how long?"

I shrugged. "However long it takes."

She sat back down and glanced at Hal, then back at me. "Okay," she said, "a couple of days, but I want to know what I'm getting into first."

I sighed and rubbed my eyes.

"Wish I could tell you, Rhea. Thing is, I don't really know myself."

*

The last thing I said to Rhea wasn't exactly true; I knew what I had to do, I just wasn't too sure of how to go about it now that Jerry was dead.

As the afternoon wore on, Hal became worried that we'd be found, and suggested that we try to find somewhere neutral, a location that no one, least of all Roller, knew about. He gave me a .45 automatic with two spare magazines and tried to offer another pistol to Rhea, but she turned it down.

"I'd take it if I were you," he said to her. "We don't know how tricky this situation's going to get."

Rhea shook her head before pulling on her greatcoat. "No, thanks. I'll leave the guns to you boys." As we watched, she strapped the magnetic scabbard to her leg, clicked the machete in place and covered it with her coat. She looked up at us. "Well? Shall we?"

Hal brought along a holdall which, aside from a few clothes and other bits and pieces, held a shotgun with extra cartridges. Trying to look as casual and relaxed as possible, we left his house and got into his car.

That was when the shooting started.

Chapter Six

There was the crack of a powerful rifle and the wing mirror on my side exploded, glass and plastic spraying over the street and the bonnet of the car. All three of us turned to look at the side of the road, stupidly losing seconds to scan the houses opposite until Hal saw the culprit.

"Shit!" he said, pointing over to the porch of one house. A man sat hunkered down, a large rifle in his hands, the butt against his shoulder as he stared down the telescopic sight at us. His clothing, standard-issue Kevlar, was matte black with the exception of a white Maltese cross over the left breast.

"Church Police," I said, recognising the insignia just as the windshield starred and the rear-view mirror shattered, spraying Hal and me with slivers of glass.

"Ow, fuck!" he shouted, running his hand over his face and coming away with smears of blood. "He fucking shot me!"

Rhea suddenly leaned over the seats and grabbed Hal's shoulder. "Drive, you idiot!" The rifleman fired again as Hal started the car and pulled out as quick as he could, smacking the parked car in front, our headlight and its rear light giving up the ghost. Glancing out of my window, I saw the rifleman speaking into what could only be the mike of his headset, nonchalantly watching us as we drove off.

"There's going to be more," I said as Hal finally found the accelerator and sent us squealing away from his house.

"Good, I could do with getting some of the bastards back for shooting up my car." He braked suddenly as a large black van, the side adorned with another Maltese cross, pulled out and stopped in front of us, side on. Hal turned left, almost rolling the car, and I glanced back to find the van now following us, its sirens and lights quiet for some reason. "Bastards!" Hal screamed as another van pulled out as we neared the next junction. Again Hal turned, this time right, the second van now following behind the first.

"Ever get the feeling we're being herded?" Rhea said. I agreed with her. Hal said something, but his words were drowned out by the voice of God from above.

"STOP THE CAR! THROW YOUR WEAPONS OUT AND STEP AWAY FROM THE VEHICLE!"

I stuck my head out of the window just as a searchlight was flicked on, illuminating the late afternoon and startling me slightly, but not before I saw a Church Police helicopter flying almost silently above us, the white cross stark against the black underbelly of the thing. Someone was leaning out of the side, a bullhorn held up to his mouth.

"YOU ARE UNDER ARREST! STOP YOUR CAR AND SURRENDER!"

Rhea stuck her head forward again and smiled at me as if I were stupid. "I don't like guns, but you've got one. You wanna use it?" she asked sweetly, her smile replaced by a frown as she finished. I thought for a very brief second: I was almost certainly wanted by the Church Police and the RAF in connection with Jerry's death and the death of the mugger; there was a gangster after me because I might have linked him to the same crimes; and then were the Downers. They might have just been insulted at first, but with one of them now less an arm, I'd guess they were pretty pissed off with me as well.

"Fuck it," I said and pulled out the .45. Leaning out of the window as far as I dared, I aimed up at the helicopter and let off a couple of shots. I didn't expect to hit anything, which was just as well because I didn't, but I grinned as the copter pulled up sharply. I turned my attention to the vans following us just as Hal yelled and turned again. As we roared off down a side street, another van zipped past me before joining the chase. Once again we had been moved into the street that they wanted us in.

I aimed at the first van again, only to see one of the Church Police marksmen standing in the doorway, belted to the cab, rifle in hand, steadying himself for the shot. I fired wildly, pointing the pistol in the general direction of the van. The rifleman didn't even flinch. He fired once and I saw a huge hole appear in the bodywork above the rear wheel, shards of metal flying into the road. He calmly took aim again, fired a second time and another hole was ripped into the car a few inches away from the first one.

"They're trying to shoot out the tyre," I said, squeezing back inside the car. Images of the tyre exploding, the car rolling and me still half in, half out of the car ran through my head.

"Well, fucking stop them!" Hal screamed, looking around for a new turning, somewhere the Church Police wouldn't be lying in wait for us. With one hand he reached into the holdall and handed me the shotgun. More shots came from behind us.

"STOP THE CAR! THROW OUT YOUR WEAP- ONS! YOU ARE UNDER ARREST!"

The helicopter was obviously back, descending just as I leaned out of the window again, pointing rather than aiming the shotgun at the lead van. I saw the driver's expression change to a look of surprise crossing over his features as he saw what I had, quickly replaced by one of rage and indignation. The van accelerated and lunged at us; the rifleman staggered in the doorway, caught off guard as the driver intended to ram us before I could fire. He wasn't fast enough. I fired once, the window of the van turning white as the glass cracked and splintered madly. My second shot burst through the windscreen, making the front of the van seem to disintegrate in one mad instant. Again, I saw the driver, his hands clutching at his throat as he tried to stop the gouts of blood that sprayed the interior of the cab. The steering wheel tilted, the van turned sharply and the whole thing spun, falling on to its side, crushing the rifleman who still stood, leaning out, trying to aim at us. There was a brief scream though I couldn't tell whether that was the tyres or the marksman as he disappeared beneath the metal. The van quickly tipped over on to its roof, sliding down the road.

The second van burst through it, a great belch of flame coming from the first van's engine as it exploded, debris scattering over the road and the cars parked on either side.

Hal screamed and swerved as, from the side of the street, some idiot pedestrian stepped out. The car leaned to the left, Hal hauling on the wheel with one hand, flashing a V at the man with the other. Behind us, the two remaining Church Police vans still followed, a rifleman leaning out of the door of the nearest as if he were a clone of his now-dead comrade.

More shots rang out, mixed with the returning sounds of the helicopter. "Aitch, fucking sort that out," Hal yelled, driving down the impossibly clear street. As we passed a turn-off, I noticed barriers and wheel spikes laid across it. The Church Police had known where we were and had taken the time to cut off any route except the one they wanted us to take. "Aitch, for fuck's sake!" Hal shouted, snapping me back to reality.

I leaned out of the car again, firing up at the helicopter with the .45, grinning as two of my shots sparked off the bottom of the thing, before I realised it was bulletproof.

"SURRENDER YOUR WEAPONS! THERE IS NO WAY OUT!"

The rifleman in the van fired off another few shots, one of which blew out the rear window, covering Rhea in glass, before exploding through the front. The bullets used by the Church Police each contained a tiny piece of glycerin; when the bullet was fired, the glycerin was forced to the rear of the casing by the acceleration. Upon impact, as the bullet rapidly decelerated, the glycerin was thrown forward to hit the relatively soft head which then exploded outward, tearing the target to shreds. They were designed to explode when they hit a substantial target — like a human body — and not glass. We were lucky it didn't blow up until it left the car.

"Hal, we're driving exactly where they want us to!" Rhea said as I crawled back in, ejecting the spent magazine from my .45 and loading another.

"There's nowhere else to go!" Hal shouted back, not taking his eyes from the road. "All the side roads are blocked!"

"Then turn around," Rhea said calmly. "Go back the way we came."

Hal and I glanced at each other, then at Rhea. The next second Hal grabbed the hand brake, turned the wheel madly and spun the car so it faced in the opposite direction. Before I could register them, both vans had shot past us while Hal accelerated, knocking off the brake and charging back up the long road we'd just come down.

"STOP YOUR CAR! SURRENDER NOW AND YOU WON'T BE HURT! STOP NOW!" For the first time it sounded as if a note of desperation had slipped into the voice behind the megaphone. Rhea and I watched through the remains of the rear window as the large, cumbersome vans tried to turn around. They rammed parked cars on either side, clumsily performing six- or seven-point turns, all the while receding in the distance. A moment later and we drove through the burning shell of the first van, the driver and rifleman fortunately hidden by the smoke that billowed from the wreck.

More shots cracked through the afternoon air, gouging holes in the bonnet of Hal's car as the helicopter's gunman fired down on us. Something in our engine sparked, smoked, then burst into flames, turning the front of the car into an earthbound comet.

"Fuck! I can't see!" Hal said as dark smoke flew back over the shattered windscreen.

"STOP THE CAR! THROW DOWN YOUR WEAPONS AND SURRENDER!"

"Can't that bloke say anything else?" I said, peering up through the smoke.

Rhea wound down her window, cursing all the time under her breath. She reached into one of her pockets and, after a moment of searching, pulled out a round, black object the size of a tennis ball. By pressing some part of it, she caused it to split apart on its axis, creating a gap about half an inch wide revealing small red lights flickering off and on. I watched her count to three, then lean out of the window and fling the ball up at the helicopter.

The explosion tore over us and I gaped as the roof of the car dented, bulging inward as the shock wave slammed down on it, extinguishing the flames on the front of the car. My ears popped and for a moment I could hardly breathe. The air, when I gasped for it, was hot and burned my throat. A second later the world turned to fire. Flames descended in waves, pushed out and down by the blast, wrapping us in heat. All three of us yelled as they poured through the open and shattered windows, kissing us briefly like lovers on a summer vacation before disappearing.

More explosions burst behind us as the helicopter fell from the sky, dropping on to the parked cars on the left of the road. It ignited them, reminding me of the fireworks I dimly remembered from a time before Bonfire Night was abandoned. One after another the cars exploded, the windows of the houses shattering in the blasts.

I looked at Rhea. "What the fuck was that?"

She ignored the question and leaned forward to speak to Hal. "We need to ditch this car. It's too conspicuous."

"No shit?" he said with a grin. We drove past Hal's house, and saw that the Church rifleman who had been across the street was now gone.

"Is there anywhere nearby you can get rid of this thing?"

Hal chuckled as if he hadn't just been in a car chase or been shot at dozens of times. He glanced back at her.

"Trust me."

*

He drove us through the same streets that he had the night before, dodging the ever watchful Church cameras. With the November evening dropping down around us quickly and lights flickering on along the roadside, we were struck with a sense of *déjà vu*, as if we had suddenly driven into last night and were even now escaping from a shrieking, amputated Downer. Hal drove serenely, a smile on his lips, his fingers tapping to the beat of a song he was whistling, high on an adrenaline rush. Rhea sat in the back, watching the few people that were out, most of them returning from work, their briefcases as heavy as their expressions. I sat in the front, unable to stop thinking about the firefight, and the deaths and destruction we had caused, and smoked one cigarette after another.

The city rumbled along as it had for years, on the outside barely changed since the advent of the Godhead. People still worked for their living, still caught the Underground or drove into the city and slaved away in soul-stealing shops or spirit-crushing offices, only to return at the close of day to the family home. There they'd sit and eat, watching the few government-approved programmes or re-runs of safe sitcoms and early soap operas, selected for their lack of sex, violence or social issues. At least the majority of people seemed to. The few teenagers around still went out and got pissed, and there remained the vestiges of an underground where people such as Hal and Roller operated; in the case of the latter, they could indulge their egos and set themselves up as gang leaders or heads of organised crime. Such two-bit criminals had made good for themselves in the years since the Godhead was elected.

And then, of course, there were the Uppers and Downers.

"Here we go," Hal said, pulling into the large courtyard of an old service station. A big woman looked out at us from the well-lit cashier's desk that was situated in little more than a shed, a cigarette between her lips, her stained white T-shirt stretched over her breasts which hung like water-filled balloons down her front. With some difficulty she eased her bulk out from behind the desk and over to the door leading out onto the foyer. She cupped her hands around her face, and peered out at us then opened the door and stuck her head out.

"All right, May?" Hal shouted to her, leaning out of his window. "Is Spud around?"

"That you, Hal?" May called back, her cigarette bobbing up and down with her words. Hal said that it was. "He's round the back. 'Ang on and I'll open the gate." She ducked back inside and waddled around to her seat. Presumably she must have flicked a switch or pushed a button because off to one side, part of a corrugated iron fence slid back, rattling on its runners. Hal tooted his horn in thanks and slowly drove the car through.

We entered another forecourt, much like the one at Roller's warehouse that I'd visited the day before; oil and water, metal and rubber, the smells of a working man's garage, a place where engines were taken apart, tampered with and rebuilt daily. An alien place to me. I knew how to drive, could replace the oil; hell, I could even change a tyre. Anything more complex than that was lost on me.

The three of us stepped out of the ruined car after Hal

had pulled up and watched as a young guy walked over to us, grinning beneath his number-two haircut and wiping his greasy hands on his combat trousers.

"How you doing, fella?" he asked Hal, shaking his hand.

"Not too bad, mate, apart from this fucking thing." Hal indicated the car.

"What's up with it?" Spud asked, nodding to me and Rhea as he passed us. "Shit, I can see what's wrong with it," he said, kneeling down and poking at the large bullet holes in the side. "Who did it?"

"Church Police," Hal said. Spud whistled.

"Why don't you guys go grab us something to eat off May? I'm starving," Hal said, turning to us. He nodded to me when I frowned. Obviously he and his friend had some things to sort out.

Rhea and I walked over to the gate through which we'd driven. It had closed behind us but there was a small door cut into the fence beside it. Stepping through, we walked over to May's hut.

"You friends of Hal's then?" she asked as we walked into the tiny store. I smiled at her and headed for the small fridge which held a selection of rolls, sandwiches, pasties and drinks fit only for famine sufferers. I refrained from choosing anything for myself, but picked up something which declared itself to be a corned beef and potato pasty for Hal; we'd soon see how hungry he was.

"Hal got himself into trouble, has he?" May asked, before looking back at the puzzle she was trying to complete. It was one of those that had a grid of squares, each containing a number, with each number corresponding to a letter. All May had to do was work out what letters went where (the magazine gave her three to start with) and fill in the rest of the grid. The way she was chewing her pen and frowning down at the page made me wonder how long she'd been working on it.

Rhea stood by the rack of government-approved, or at least goverment tolerated, newspapers, flicking through one or two. The murder of the archbishop was hardly mentioned, even though it had only happened a couple of days ago; the real news, it seemed, was which pop star was marrying which footballer. With all the changes that had taken place in this country — hell, in the whole world — it still made me wince that the best investigative journalism had to offer was tales of celebrities enjoying the fifteen minutes of fame afforded them by their artificial lives.

"Is that it, love?" May asked as I placed the pasty on the counter.

"Unless you've got anything fit for humans to eat," I said before I could stop myself.

"You cheeky sod! If you don't want it — "

"Oh, shut up," I said wearily, far too tired to bother with an overweight, retarded shopkeeper. I gave her the money for the pasty and walked out, Rhea following.

"What was that about?" she asked me, handing me a cigarette. The petrol pumps on the forecourt looked as if they hadn't been used since the combustion engine was first invented, so I took the fag and lit it up.

"I'm just tired. Seems like I haven't stopped since Saturday night." I glanced back at the shop window; May had returned to her poor man's crossword. "Everything just seems to be a bit fucked up right now,"

Without a word Rhea guided me away from the door in the fence, over to the other side of the dimly lit court. Glancing around first, she turned back to me.

"Aitch, can I ask you something?"

"Sure."

"Do you trust Hal?"

"Of course I do. He's a mate of mine." I said, remembering the conversation I'd had with Hal earlier.

"A mate you haven't seen for a few years and who happens to work for a gangster who's now after you."

"A mate who happened to save our necks last night and today," I said.

Rhea shook her head. "*I* saved our necks today. It was my idea to turn the car round and it was my thermal concussion grenade that brought the copter down. Last night? Don't you think it was just a bit convenient that Hal was staking out your mate's place?"

I puffed angrily on my cigarette. "He said himself he was waiting to see if I turned up. Roller was trying to find me and Hal wanted to let me know." I jabbed my finger at her as I made my point. "He's my friend and I trust him. And now, if you don't mind," I added, flicking ash from my cigarette into the evening, the wind snatching it away, "I'm going to give him his pasty."

I stalked off, heading for the door, when Rhea laughed, emitting a burst of throaty chuckles. Turning back to her, I frowned, then grinned myself. As an exit line from an argument, it left a lot to be desired.

We looked at each other, me smiling, her still sniggering.

"Sorry," I said. "Like I said, I'm tired."

Rhea stepped over to me.

"Hey, don't hassle it. You're paying me to stick around, remember. For that I'll deal with the occasional temper tantrum."

"That's so nice to know," I said. Together we walked back to the door in the fence.

Hal still stood with his friend Spud, but they were now looking over a different car, a small, inconspicuous family vehicle. This didn't encourage me at all; if we got into trouble again like we had that afternoon, I wanted something fast that we could rely upon. As we stepped over, Hal frowning dubiously at the pasty I gave him, the shrill sound of a mobile phone interrupted the over zealous adjectives that Spud was using to describe to the car. He stopped and reached into his trouser pocket, pulling out his mobile.

"Yeah? Yeah, he's here, hang on." With a shrug he handed the phone over to Hal.

"Hello? Roller, hi, how you doing?" Hal glanced at me, pulling a face which basically said *oh shit*. "No, I haven't seen him . . . no, saw him Saturday with you and . . . uh huh . . . yeah, sure . . . sure, got you . . . yeah, no worries . . . all right, Roller, yeah, I'll catch you later." Hal turned the phone off and returned it to Spud. He stepped over to me and Rhea. "Roller asked me if I'd seen you," he whispered.

"I kind of guessed that," I said. "What did he sound like?"

"Fine. He said if I saw you to ask you to get in touch."

"Like that's gonna happen," I said.

"You'd be surprised at what's going to happen, Mr McKean."

I turned around to face the speaker. Roller stood next to the door in the fence, mobile in hand, the Pale Man and a couple of his soldiers next to him, all armed.

"You know, I'm not surprised at all," I said, then ran like hell.

Chapter Seven

It's amazing how much your perceptions can change in only a small amount of time.

I woke up in what first appeared to be nothing more than a white blur; my eyes weren't focusing for a while and nothing was defined, and it looked like I was entirely surrounded by cotton wool. Someone — a nurse, I presumed — found me awake at some point after that and, even though I asked her where I was and who she was, she did nothing except tighten the sheets around me, tucking them under the edge of the bed to stop me moving. I screamed at her as she walked away, indifferent to my suffering and I eventually slipped back into unconsciousness, withdrawing from the harsh, sterile white world into the comfort and warmth of blackness.

The next time I surfaced I spent ten minutes thanking a God I didn't believe in for the fact that my eyesight had returned to normal; since childhood, I had been scared of going blind, of being deprived of the world around. I stopped praying when whatever medication I was on wore off and pain insinuated itself into my body.

My head pounded. Every heartbeat sent a crushing throb of agony around, over and through my skull. My right leg, I realised now, was suspended outside the bed by a system of pulleys and coated in a thick plaster cast. It itched constantly, yet I had no way of reaching to scratch it, to salve the sensation of fiery ants eating away at my bones. My chest stung with every breath, my lungs like fleshy beehives with the inhabitants at home, the bandage around me tight and uncaring of my need to inhale. My left arm, like my chest, was bandaged, and while it didn't itch, I could feel a wetness between my skin and the cloth as if it were slowly melting, like a gauze-wrapped candle placed beneath a grill. I tried to call for a nurse, my rough, dry throat coughing out the words. No one came.

For perhaps an hour, perhaps only ten minutes, I lay in the bed, hurting, aching, itching, and the only companion I had was my pain.

Again a nurse appeared at some point, though by then I had drifted out of my body. My conscious self had had enough of the pitiful whining and crying of my body as it repaired itself, and had decided to rise above it all. I remember being aware of the nurse doing something to the drip which fed into my hand, but I didn't take any active part in it. I'd read about so-called out-of-body experiences but this was different. I wasn't on the ceiling looking back at my body; if anything, I was deeper within my mind than at any other time in my life. I understood everything that had gone on around me, and knew that what I was planning to do, what I had to do, was the only way I could go. My world would continue only so far if I relinquished my goal, my quest, my Grail. It was with a profound sadness that I realised I was sliding back into unconsciousness again. In my new-found state of self awareness with the sense of religious importance my mind had attached to my goal, I no longer wished to use the dark realm as an escape route. But by that point I had no choice.

Eventually, with only the faintest, saddest memory of my experiences within myself, I returned to normal.

*

Rhea was at the bedside when I came round. As I stirred, she looked up from the book she was reading and smiled ruefully.

"How you doing?"

I gulped a couple of times, trying to get my throat back in working order, but it didn't seem to help. She reached over to the ubiquitous bedside cabinet that every hospital bed has and poured me a beaker of water from the plastic jug. I sipped at it, tasting what could have been week old dust floating in it but grateful nonetheless.

"Where am I?" I asked after a few sips. Running my tongue over my lips and the inside of my mouth, I could feel dry, sore patches and peeling skin. "How long have I been here?"

Rhea took a cigarette from her pocket. She still wore the same long coat that seemed to hold all of her wordly possessions, most of them lethal in one way or another. She lit her fag with a match and inhaled deeply.

"You're somewhere safe, I'll tell you that," she said, blowing smoke out of her nose in two thin streams like a dieting dragon. "And you've been here for close on five weeks,"

I stared at her, not saying anything. She smoked in silence, staring back at me.

"What happened?" I managed to ask.

"You don't remember?" I shook my head weakly. "Hardly surprising, the crack on the head you took." She sighed and rubbed at her head as if bringing her own memories to the fore.

"Roller turned up, you remember that much, yeah?" I nodded. "You tried running, I tried following you, then Roller's arseholes decided to turn the place into a bullet festival." Rhea looked at me, her voice neutral and matter-of-fact as if she were reporting a news item. "Hal's dead. He got hit almost immediately. His friend, the mechanic, went down as well. You and me, we ran into the scrapyard and came up against a fence. You gave me a lift over and as I was hanging over the top, reaching down to pull you up, Roller and his men caught up with us. One of them smacked you round the head with the butt of a shotgun and you just collapsed. Then he looked at me, aimed his pistol and the Pale Man shot him."

I could do nothing except stare and frown at her.

Rhea shrugged. "The Pale Man, the Upper, stepped up beside Roller, put a pistol against his head and blew his brains out. The other guys didn't know what to do, and while they were deciding, he shot them all. Every single one." She crushed her barely smoked cigarette out on the floor, stamping on it and rubbing at the bridge of her nose as she did so before looking up at me again. "It was fucking weird, Aitch. He shot them all quite calmly, one after another, then looked up at me. I was still leaning over the top of the fence and I was positive I was next. He shot them, then blew me a kiss and walked away."

We stared at each other again. The sounds of what I took to be other rooms on the ward drifted through the door of my own. Voices were raised occasionally; metal pans and trolleys clanked or squeaked; a muted television set played a programme I might once have recognised.

"Hal's dead?" I said, not really meaning it to be a question.

"'Fraid so," Rhea answered. "Once I got over my shock, I jumped back down into the scrap-yard, picked you up and carried you out to the car Hal's mate was going to sell or trade us. I drove out into the garage, looked around for the Pale Man but couldn't see him." She shook her head sadly. "They killed the woman in the shop as well. She was on the forecourt, just lying there. She still had her puzzle book in one hand."

"Shit," I whispered, still trying to comprehend the idea that Hal was dead. Granted, over the last few years we hadn't been in touch, what with me being out of the country, but we'd grown up together, we'd been bought by the same man. And now, as with Jerry, I'd caused his death.

"There was nothing you could have done, Aitch," Rhea said kindly. "You know that, so don't go blaming yourself."

I sniffed back the tears that threatened to spill over my cheeks, wiping my nose with my good hand. "Yeah, I guess so. Doesn't make it any easier though, does it?"

Rhea knew enough not to answer that sort of question and we were quiet for a while, her sat in the chair, me practically immobile in the bed. After a few minutes I pointed at my arm and leg. "If all I got from Roller's crew was a smack on the head, how comes I ended up like this?"

She smiled again and couldn't help chuckling slightly.

"When it comes to a high-speed car chase, I'm nowhere near as good a driver as Hal was. I drove out of the garage and ran smack-bang into a car full of Downers." She shrugged. "God knows if they were looking for us or were just a bunch of bastards joy riding; either way, no sooner had I pulled off than they instantly followed, ramming the car. I speeded up, they speeded up, you know how these things go. Christ knows how I managed to lose them, but I did. Thing is, I'd turned into a dead-end lane and before I could stop, we smacked right into the wall."

Rhea looked at me, a guilt-laden smile on her lips. "I'd

Rhea looked at me, a guilt-laden smile on her lips. "I'd buckled up my seat belt when I got in the car. Sadly..."

"You forgot to put mine on," I finished for her. She nodded and poured herself a beaker of water from the jug.

"Sorry, Aitch. We smashed into the wall, and while I got off with a bump on the head, you practically went through the windscreen. The bandage is on your arm because, before I could get out and drag you out of the car, a fire had started and your arm was right in it. Even that didn't wake you up. Anyway, one way or another, I managed to get you here."

I looked round the room again, remembering the vague sight of it I'd had when I'd woken with blurred vision. Like any other hospital I'd been in either as a patient or as a visitor, it was pure, sterile white. The only time colour ever invaded places like this was when relatives brought flowers or blood was dripped on to the floor. I was confused, though; hospitals didn't admit just anyone to a private room. You took a ticket when you got into casualty and you waited your turn. If you happened to die before a doctor, nurse, intern or janitor was able to see you . . . well, it just speeded up the queue for those behind you.

"Where is here?" I asked.

"The St Mary of Bethlehem Hospital, established 1982 by Sir Edward Wilcox," she said with a smile. "He owed me a favour, so I was able to get the room. You, however, have been paying for it the whole time you've been here." She reached into the cabinet and pulled out my rucksack. "I kinda guessed you wanted to keep this after all you'd been through to get it." She opened one of the pockets and produced the envelope containing the remains of my money, which looked to be a couple of hundred pounds. "Sorry, Aitch, but the favour was getting the room, not paying for it."

"Shit," I whispered again. "How long have I got left in here?"

"Another day. This time tomorrow, you're back on the streets." She shoved my rucksack back into the cabinet and stood, taking another cigarette from her packet. "And so am I. You've been paying me on retainer as well, remember, and, as you're almost broke, I'm out of here. See you round."

"Wait a second! You're leaving me here?" I tried sitting up, then collapsed back, hissing through my teeth as my body decided to remind me why I was in this bed. "I need you, Rhea."

She stopped at the door, looking over at me. "Aitch, I'll be honest with you: while you've been comatose, I've been through the entire contents of that rucksack, and I can't find one damn thing that seems worth going back to a house and getting jumped by a Downer for. I don't know what you've got planned because you won't tell me. There is nothing in there that's going to make any sort of difference to anyone or anything, with the exception of what *was* a large wad of cash and which isn't anymore." She stepped back over to the bed. "Tell me what's so damn important you're willing to risk your life for it."

"Rhea, I can't — "

"Whoa, hold on. I'll admit I'm intrigued. I want to know what the big secret is, and so I'm going to give you one last chance. I don't want to hear any bullshit about how you can't tell me anything. You tell me everything, or I'm going, it's as simple as that. No stalling, no hedging; you tell me or I go. What's it gonna be, Aitch?"

I sighed, closed my eyes and silently cursed her.

"Okay, sit down. I'll tell you. But only if you agree to help me."

"No. I'll decide after you tell me, not before." Rhea sat down, crossed her legs and looked at me. "Well?"

"God, you're a hard woman," I said. I took a deep breath and began.

*

"Most of what Hal told us back at his flat is basically true. Since the Godhead came to power, he's effectively been converting everyone to his own brand of Christianity, never claiming, but never denying, to be divine himself. If the people view him as a new Messiah, as Christ reborn, then that can't hurt his public image. Whether or not there is a Heaven or Hell doesn't really matter. I don't know whether it's as black and white as that, or if there's a more . . . I don't know, philosophical argument to take into account. Either way, the end result is the same: people die every day, by natural causes or otherwise. Those who are "good", who believe in the religion that the Godhead has corrupted, cause one of the characters known as Uppers to be created when they die. At the same time, the "bad" guys, the unbelievers, spawn Downers. Whatever you may think about the religious aspects of the thing, there's no denying that the Downers appear to be the product of some kind of Hell.

"The new Christianity has really taken off, and it's no surprise, because its proponents tell everyone that the Uppers are basically angels on Earth and the Downers are the opposite. Normal people, the everyday folk, they see a Downer and they can't help but wonder how he got like that, his skin burnt and cracked, constantly smouldering. The only thing they can come up with is Hell. Most people don't want to go to Hell, especially when they see the result of visiting it, so they embrace the Godhead's religion, eager to be saved when they die.

"I don't know how Hal found out, but the stuff he said about there being no births over the last ten years . . . it's true. Hospitals will deny it point-blank; some will even create new figures and statistics saying that births have been on the decrease since the eighties just to cover it up. No one has been born since the Godhead arrived, give or take a few months either way. The only people left alive now are the ones who were already around when he turned up."

I stopped for a moment, drinking from the beaker of water Rhea had poured for me.

"About five years ago, I left Britain. I got into some trouble with the law — what used to be the law, before the Church Police and the RAF finally took it over — and I had to get out for a while. I went to America, bumming around for the most part until I met up with a bunch of guys who called themselves the Church of the Real American People." I laughed quietly. "They hadn't really thought about what their initials spelt out," I explained to Rhea when she asked me what I was chuckling about.

"Anyhow, these guys, despite their poorly thought-out name, actually had their heads screwed on. They had access to all sorts of stuff on the net, before it started being censored and doctored by the federal agencies, and a lot of it proved that there were no more children being born, at least as far as anything like that could be proved." I paused for a moment, thinking back to the time I had spent with them, camped out in the Midwest, hanging out with Native Americans, people I used to call Red Indians when I was a kid. "They were a pretty cool bunch — a little stereotyped as only ageing American hippies can be, but they were mainly on the ball. We spent a fair amount of time stoned out of our heads, doing acid and peyote and all sorts of shit, messing our heads up with hallucinogenics." I sighed wistfully. "Great times, they were . . .

"The situation with the Uppers and Downers wasn't as bad over there as it is here or in Europe. None of us really knew why, but the theory we came up with was that whenever someone died, an Upper or a Downer was created; they then appeared somewhere in the world, and the reason there seemed to be less of both types in the States was that there was more space for them to appear in. Here, it was obvious we'd soon be swamped with them, but over there it was several years before they began to make any serious impact on the country. The media picked up on them, but they were treated as bizarre items to be reported on, sort of like the alien thing years back. People were actually claiming to have been abducted by Uppers, and said that they were the source of the Greys and the flying saucers.

"Everything came to an end, though. The CIA, the ATF, the FBI . . . they all began breaking up any sort of community like ours with increasing regularity. It was only about a year later that stories of the Downers' involvement in the government over there began to appear, but I don't really think it was anything to do with them. The US top dogs have never liked people thinking for themselves.

"Just before we all broke up, though, the head of the Church, a crazy guy calling himself Broken Feather even though there wasn't a hint of Indian blood in his veins, claimed to have discovered the purpose of our new earthly companions, namely, that they were readying themselves for war. More and more, he claimed, both Uppers and Downers were working themselves into positions of power, either openly, as in the case of those Uppers who worked as advisors to state senators, or secretly. Downers, he thought, were the real secretive ones; with the way they looked, the public just couldn't find them trustworthy. According to Broken Feather, though, military contractors and agencies were snapping up Downers left, right and centre, using whatever knowledge they possessed to help develop new weapons." I shrugged as best I could. "I don't know if that's true — the bloke was almost completely paranoid — but it's certainly a possibility. With our group disbanded, and with the last piece of evidence he gave me, I decided to come back to Britain and try something ridiculously stupid." I looked over at Rhea.

"I'm going to try to destroy the Godhead."

She stared at me for a while, her chin resting in one hand. "How did I know you were going to say that?" she asked.

"Broken Feather and some of the others captured an Upper. They drove into the nearest town one day, which was about fifty miles away, and found a bunch of locals giving this guy a hard time, pushing him around, throwing things at him, typical stuff like that, you know? Broken Feather convinced him they could give him a ride out of town to a place where he'd be okay, and could get some rest before he went on his way.

"No sooner were they halfway back to the camp than they pulled over and beat the shit out of him, tied him up and brought him back for everyone else to see." I closed my eyes, remembering the conquering heroes, the victorious hunters as they drove through the ramshackle wooden gates, the body of an Upper tied over the hood of their truck, his head hanging over one side, banging unconsciously against the car with every bump and jolt it took.

"It was hideous. The entire camp came to look, myself included, and we watched as Broken Feather and the other guys tied this poor bastard up to a tree, hanging him from his wrists so his feet were just on the ground. They sprayed him with a hose to wake him up, then everyone had a chance to walk past him, staring at him, poking him with sticks or their fingers, trying to work out what he was.

"They're different from us; with Downers, the differences are obvious, but Uppers are more subtle. They're taller, in general; I don't think I've ever seen one shorter than about six foot six, but there's more than that. With the exception of what's on their heads, they have no hair. The guy they hung up from the tree was stripped naked after a while. He had no nipples, no genitals, no navel. His skin was pure white, as well, with no coloration at all, and it *felt* different. You can put your hand on an Upper and feel as if you're touching the surface of a pond beneath tight, thin plastic; it's cool and pliable. If you pushed hard enough, you got the impression that your hand would just go straight through.

"They cut him, eventually. The poor son of a bitch was screaming at them, wondering what they wanted to know, even though he swore he knew nothing about anything, but they never even asked him any questions. They were like a bunch of kids in a biology lesson, left to dissect frogs on their own; they knew they had to open him up to find out how he worked, but they had no idea what they were looking for or what it was that they found."

I drank again from the beaker, draining it and asking Rhea to pour me another. I hadn't thought of that Upper for years, and it was disconcerting just how vividly the memory came back to me.

"They stuck a knife in his stomach first. I don't know what they expected — probably blood and guts like any normal human, but Uppers are different in so many ways. The knife went into him easily and he screamed.

"Light streamed from the wound; bright, white light that made us all cover our eyes and left dark reflections dancing in our vision. As it dimmed, we looked back at him. He hung there, obviously dead, the wound clean with no blood and only the faintest glimmer of the light, which quickly faded away.

Broken Feather kept cutting him, again and again, but nothing else happened, and nothing came out of him. He may as well have been slicing away at an empty bag.

"Not long after that, the camp was raided by the ATF, broken up, and I came back here."

Rhea looked at me as she ground out her cigarette in the ashtray and I realised that, for the first time since I was twelve, I didn't want one.

"As grim as that is, it doesn't explain why you want to kill the Godhead," she said.

"Broken Feather was paranoid, like I said. That's why he had to find out what the Upper was. Trouble was, he didn't know the best way to go about it, and the poor sod just ended up dead. As far as getting stuff off the Internet goes, though, there was no one better than Broken Feather. After he'd killed the Upper, he spent most of his time on his PC, talking with other people all over the world about what he'd seen, desperate for information. That's when he stumbled across the stuff about the births and the hospitals. He also found out something about the guy over here who called himself the Godhead. Not only had he built a new religion on the foundations of the old one, but he was speeding up the process of creating Uppers."

I sat up in my bed, painfully, and stared at Rhea.

"Since almost day one, he's been recruiting, converting and killing the people of Britain. He's got Christian concentration camps all over the country, on Salisbury Plain, Dartmoor, up in Scotland and in Wales, places nobody goes to these days. He's taking the converted masses to these places, probably with promises of relocation and good jobs, and slaughtering them so that more and more Uppers will appear throughout the world, some of them obviously in Britain. He's preparing for war by killing us."

I slumped back in my bed, trying not to think of the huge number of people who, week in, week out, were being carted off to remote areas and killed just so that the Godhead could lay claim to more of his tall, pale soldiers.

Rhea stood up and walked to the window, staring out into the hazy sunshine. From outside my room came sounds of nurses on their rounds; patients crying out for attention; doctors crying out for patience. Eventually she sighed and, without turning to me, asked,

"So what's in your bag that's so important?"

I chuckled and asked her to pass it to me. As she watched, intrigued despite herself, I unzipped the front pocket and pulled out a small box, the sort of thing engagement rings used to be sold in back in the good old days. Without a word I handed it to her. Leaning against the window sill, Rhea opened the hinged box and looked inside.

"It's a disk," she said. Wrapped in a small plastic envelope was a silver mini-disk which she held up to the dim light that filtered through the window. "I saw it in there when I went through the bag. What's on it?"

"Information, dates, proof." She looked over at me. "About the births, the camps, the Godhead's plans, the Uppers, the Downers, everything. As much information as Broken Feather could get off the net is stored on that disc; some of it's about the Americans, some of it's about Britain and Europe. It shows that the stuff that's happening here is happening throught the world. Publicly here, but more covert in the States."

Rhea stared at me, placing the disk back in its box and putting that back in the rucksack. "Everyone knows the Uppers and Downers are taking over the place, Aitch. It's common news. What good is a disk going to be? How are you going to kill the Godhead with that?"

"There are resistance groups, Rhea, dotted all over the place, some of them here in London. Jerry was supposed to introduce me to someone who could use that information."

She lit a final cigarette, crushed the empty packet and dropped it in the bin. "You're living in a dream world, Aitch. You've read or heard or seen too many things about conspiracies and world domination. You think you're going to be a great rebel commander when all you're really going to be is broken and lost." She walked to the door, opened it and looked back at me.

"Thanks for the money for nothing, Aitch, but you need

help."

"Then help me!" I called as she walked off. With just a wave over her shoulder, Rhea was gone. "Shit," I whispered. I lay on my bed, staring up at the ceiling, trying not to think about the itch in my leg and the dampness beneath the bandages on my arm.

Five minutes later, as if they'd been waiting for a cue, three people walked in. Two of them wore the standard matte black uniform with white Maltese cross of the Church Police. The other, a middle-aged woman, her hair cut into a bob, wearing jeans, shirt and a loose casual jacket, walked over to my bed and picked up my rucksack. She checked the pockets, smiling when she saw the disk box, then hooked my bag over her shoulder. With her other hand, and a smile on her face, she reached into the inside pocket of her jacket and produced her wallet, flashing me her badge and ID.

"Corben, RAF. I've been wanting to have a chat with you for some time, Mr McKean," she said, patting my hand.

"Shit," I whispered again.

Chapter Eight

"How are you, Mr McKean?"

"Well, apart from the fact that my hands are both hand-cuffed to a pole behind my back, my arm smells like it's gone septic, my leg hurts like a bastard, I haven't been fed or had anything to drink for three days and I've pissed myself . . . everything's fine. How are you?"

Corben closed the door to my cell and sat in the plastic chair that had been taunting me since I'd been dragged in here. I was sat on the floor, my back resting uncomfortably against the pole that my hands were cuffed to, and my arse had gone numb after the first few hours. Sitting on a cold and wet stone floor will do that. The fact that the floor was wet because my bladder gave out on me when I'd finally fallen asleep just rounded my day off.

She smiled at me, taking a stick of gum from her top pocket. As the aroma of Juicy Fruit permeated the air around me, my mouth turned into a shower head, saliva even running down my chin.

"I like a man who can keep his sense of humour," Corben said. "Shows character."

"I'm overjoyed that I please you. That's all I want to do," I said with a sour smile.

She sat and stared at me, chewing slowly. I tried to ignore her, wait her out, but as she was the first person I'd seen in three days, I was hungry for conversation as well as food.

"What have I been charged with?" I asked.

"Nothing."

"Then why are you holding me?"

"These aren't the good old days, McKean. I can keep you here for as long as I want, for any reason I want. Amnesty International doesn't exist anymore and the Geneva Convention is just a distant memory. There's no appeal court, no social worker or solicitor to plead your case. You're here until I've finished with you.

"And I haven't even started yet."

She took the empty foil gum wrapper and neatly placed

the chewed remains of the Juicy Fruit into it, balling it up and placing it into her top pocket. The badge on her chest wobbled as she swapped the gum for a small dictaphone. Corben held it out to me and pressed PLAY.

It took me a moment to recognise it; your own voice always sounds weird when you hear it on tape. There was no doubt, though, that it was me. It was also Rhea — our conversation in the hospital room. As soon as Corben saw I'd recognised it, she stopped it and placed it back in her pocket.

"That little chat alone means I can hold you forever." She sighed and crossed one leg over the other. She was a big woman, chunky, what Hal would have described as having "plenty to grab on to", and her trousers stretched tight over her thighs as she crossed them, imprisoning her flesh in black cotton. "Treason, insurrection, a plot to commit deicide — call it what you will. There is, of course, the other stuff."

"What?" I asked her, unable to hold my tongue and spoil her teasing.

"Your finger- and palm-prints were found on the passenger seat of an abandoned car. It's owner was found a couple of days later outside the city limits, a large stab wound in his neck. Your prints were also found at Jerry Hood's house, along with the body of a Downer — he'd had his arm cut off and bled to death." She smiled and shrugged. "If you could call that stuff blood. Your friend Jerry was found dead as well; his gun had your prints on it too and while that gun hadn't killed him, it had killed the young boy next to him.

"If you're so eager to be charged with something, we can sort something out, I'm sure."

I sighed, trying to wriggle my backside, partly to become a little more comfortable, mostly just to keep the blood flowing down there.

"You said *if*. Am I going to be charged?"

"If I feel like it," Corben said. "Thing is, the tape we have of your conversation makes for quite interesting listening. I haven't spoken to her yet, but Miss Leary's remarks about going through your rucksack in an attempt to find something that you couldn't bear to leave behind were intriguing, as were your explanations about the mini-disk and the hospitals and births and everything else." She paused, took out another Juicy Fruit and began chewing. "Like I said: interesting. Complete bullshit, but interesting."

Corben stood up and began pacing the length of the small cell, her hands behind her back, resting on her big butt. "The information on that disk could, theoretically, be damaging to the Godhead, but only in a public relations way. Most of it is inaccurate, some of it completely fabricated, and all of it sadly outdated. The figures contained on it are at least six or seven years old." She stopped and looked at me. "How do you know the births haven't picked up again?"

I smiled back at her and, to the best of my limited ability in my situation, shrugged.

"It's not the disk that's important, though. It's not going to unite any sort of 'rebel gangs' even if they existed and you could get it to these hypothetical heretics. But, I'll admit, we don't seem to be able to find anything else in there that would be worth risking your neck for."

Corben sat back on the chair, crossing her legs again, chewing her gum noisily.

"Either you overestimate the importance of that outdated information . . . or there's something else in that rucksack." She winked at me. "Which is it, Aitch?"

Every now and then you'll meet someone who, during a conversation, will say something so outrageously stupid that you stand there, staring at them in disbelief.

"Why don't you find out?" I said with a grin, my smile fading as I realised just how dumb I was.

Corben leaned forward.

"Tell you what, Aitch, why don't we find out together?"

*

Rhea woke as water was thrown in her face.

She was strapped to a table with wide leather belts criss-crossing her body, but the odd thing was that the table was vertical. Her long coat was gone, leaving her only in grubby jeans, a torn T-shirt and a pair of boots that looked as if they'd crossed Africa a few times. As Corben led me into Rhea's cell, the two guards, one either side of the now-dripping prisoner, saluted, then quickly genuflected.

"As you were, gentlemen," Corben said, her hand tight around my elbow. My hands were still handcuffed behind my back, and my ankles had been shackled together, although this was hardly necessary — three days spent sitting on your arse and your legs kind of lose the inclination to walk around.

"And you're the good guys," I said to Corben, as I noticed the wide strip of silver masking tape over Rhea's mouth. Corben frowned at me, stepping over to her captive.

"No, Mr McKean. We're the RAF." She turned to Rhea and walked around the upright table as she talked, the two guards stepping away to allow her room. "I've been holding your friend here since we arrested her at the hospital. We're also holding Dr Wilcox; ignoring the waiting list and granting beds as favours isn't exactly a capital offence, but hey," she said, with a smile at me, "in for a penny, eh?"

Corben walked over to a small desk where, among other things, Rhea's machete lay. She picked it up, hefting it in her hand, gauging its weight.

"Wicked-looking thing, isn't it?" she asked me. "Could cause a hell of a lot of damage to someone who got in the way. I don't know — maybe a driver who didn't want his car stolen? Or maybe a Downer who was on the lookout for someone?" She smiled and replaced the blade, picking up instead what looked for all the world like a pair of surgical pruning shears. The handles were spring-loaded; with some effort they could be squeezed together, opening the blades. As soon as any pressure was removed, the blades would snap back, slicing off whatever was between them. Corben walked back over to Rhea and, with a hardly perceptible nod from her the two guards took up positions next to me, each one grabbing an arm.

"As I said earlier, the information on that disk is years out of date. Oh, it might cause some people to ask questions; it might be seen as an embarrassment to the Godhead, but that's nothing that couldn't be fixed." Corben brushed back the damp hair from Rhea's forehead, smiling into Rhea's wide eyes which pleaded with her. "Your friend here, as far as we can work out from the tape of your conversation, has nothing really to do with whatever mad scheme it is you're involved in. She's just a hired hand."

"That's right," I said, staring at the shears in Corben's hand. Even though I hadn't eaten for three days, my stomach growled — not in hunger, but rather in trepidation. I knew what was going to happen; so did Corben and, judging by the look in her eyes, so did Rhea. But I had to try.

"Don't do it. The disk is the only thing I was holding. I don't know anything else, and neither does Rhea. Jerry was the one who was arranging things. You know that. So don't. Don't do it."

The RAF officer smiled, holding up the shears. My gaze followed them as she lowered them deliberately, slowly, her lips peeling back wetly, revealing her bright teeth. Rhea's hands were strapped down flat against the table, strips of leather holing them in place, her fingers splayed out. Corben opened the shears and slipped them under Rhea's little finger, just below the top knuckle.

"I liked your approach in the hospital room," Corben said to her. "Not letting McKean worm out of any answers. Asking him straight questions and demanding straight replies." The pair of them looked over at me, the plump, smiling RAF inspector and the thin, terrified woman I'd involved in all of this. "So, Mr McKean, I'm going to employ the same tactic. I'm going to ask you questions; if you stall or lie, I will cut off Ms Leary's fingers, a knuckle at a time. Are we clear?"

I nodded wearily, shifting my weight off my broken leg, the guards still holding my arms.

Shink!

Rhea screamed behind the masking tape, her whole body going rigid as Corben sliced off the top of her little finger.

"That's to let you know I'm serious, Mr McKean," Corben said, her smile now replaced by a hard, cold stare. Blood began to drain from the tip of Rhea's finger as Corben opened the shears again and slid the blade underneath the first knuckle of Rhea's ring finger.

"Now then," Corben said, "shall we begin?"

*

There are fourteen knuckle joints on each hand; three each on the fingers, two on the thumb. Corben asked me questions, so many questions. Every time she didn't like my answers, or I stalled, or I couldn't answer, there was a tiny *shink!* and Rhea lost another part of a finger. She passed out several times; each time she was brought back to consciousness by Corben, at first just by dousing her with water, eventually by injecting something into her bare, sweat-soaked, shaking arm.

The table below Rhea's hand ran thick and red, the pieces of her fingers collecting on the floor, pale lumps of flesh poking out of the mess like vegetables in a thick, crimson soup. By the time Corben called a break, her shirt was as red as the table beneath Rhea's hand, and the shears were slipping in her grasp, slick with gore.

I hung, limp and exhausted, in the arms of the two stoic guards who hadn't moved since they'd taken a hold of me. They still bore me up, my own arms now tingling with pins and needles, their grip having cut off most of the circulation.

Corben opened a cooler box that sat in the corner of the room and took out a beer, popping the top of the can and drinking long and deep.

"Aaaah," she sighed, following it with a belch that shook her big frame. She placed the shears on the side and walked over to me, offering the beer. I shook my head, glancing over at Rhea.

She lay against the table, her face bathed in sweat, her hair lying flat against her skull. Her whole body shook with each slow, tortured breath that she took in through her wide nostrils. Her skin was pale and drawn and she stared at me, her eyes sunk deep in shadowy pits and with such a look of hatred that I knew if she were freed at that point, she would have killed me without a thought. On her right hand only the last segments of her four fingers remained; her thumb was missing entirely.

"You've got a strong will, McKean, I'll give you that," Corben said, taking a seat and wiping some of Rhea's blood off her hand. "You just stand there and play dumb, answering my questions with pathetic lies and stories while you force me to slice off this girl's fingers. Jesus, McKean! What sort of monster are you? What's so important to you that you'll let this girl suffer?"

"I told you — the disk was all I had. Nothing else."

"If you had nothing else, how were you going to contact these 'rebel groups' of yours? Come on, McKean, I'm giving you these questions for free."

"I've told you. Jerry was the one who was arranging everything. I don't know any of them." As my legs gave out, I sagged, but the guards instantly jogged me back up. "After Jerry died, I paid Rhea to come along with me. I just didn't want to do it on my own."

"Do what, McKean?" Corben leaned forward in her chair, the condensation from the can mixing with the blood on her hand, dripping on to the floor in pale pink tears.

Suddenly, I'd had enough. I couldn't watch this bitch of a copper mutilate the woman I'd involved in something which now had no chance of completion.

"Let me sit down," I said quietly. "Let me sit down and I'll tell you everything."

Corben grinned and nodded to the guards. One of them took my weight while the other brought over a chair from somewhere. I collapsed on to it, breaking down, sobbing uncontrollably, unable to lift my arms to wipe my tears away.

I glanced at Rhea, ready to apologise, but she'd passed out again.

Slowly, with a cracked voice thick with fatigue, pain and self-loathing, I told Corben everything she wanted to hear.

*

At certain times in my life, I've believed in God and, to the best of my knowledge, He lives in a machine. Thing is, He's got a lodger in there as well who's just as likely to pop out, if not more so. They say opposites attract.

Stuff happens. I've been in situations where it seems there's no way out — maybe not life-and-death situations, but tricky nonetheless. And sooner or later, "stuff happens" which either helps sort me out, or completely screws me up.

The situation that made me quit the country about five years ago was like that. I'd been involved with some less-than-savoury characters, who in turn had linked up with some of the first Downers to take over the criminal element where I was living. Their speciality was drugs — heroin in particular. To this day, I've no idea how the stuff is made or processed or whatever the hell they do with it. All I was concerned with at that point in my life was who to sell it to.

I can't begin to compensate for the poison that I pushed. I didn't care who bought it; I sold it to kids, teenagers, married couples, businessmen and women; if she'd asked, I would have sold it to my grandmother. Anyone who was anyone or no one — if they wanted heroin they came to me. They just dialed Aitch.

If I'd been a little more discriminating about who my buyers were, things would definitely be different. As it was, my policy of "if you've got cash, I'm selling" soon dropped me in it.

Back then, before the Church Police completely took over, the law was still the old-fashioned coppers. They still did the undercover bit, and one night, in a nightclub called the Green Lantern, I sold a five-gram bag of the finest heroin to Detective Inspector Milliner. Of course, I didn't know she was a cop until she arrested me — the handcuffs kind of gave the game away. No sooner was I wearing them than her back-up appeared, sliding out of the shadows and from behind the pillars to stand on every side of me, one each to the left, right and back. With barely a word, and making no attempt to play the scene down, they marched me toward the exit. Everyone had backed away, watching, smiling and laughing at me. Some of the people chuckling behind their watered-down beers were customers of mine. Did they care? Hell, they knew they could find another dealer in a day or two — maybe not one with my class, contacts or calibre of H, but a dealer nonetheless. And besides, it wasn't them getting arrested.

Then God stuck His face out of the machine. Or rather, His opposite did.

"Officers, can I help you?"

DI Milliner stopped in front of me. Before her, his clothes smouldering, his cigarette crisping between his lips, was a Downer. He introduced himself, and when he said his name, my ears pricked up. I'd never met him before, but my suppliers had used his name in conversation more than once. He was the Downer they bought the heroin from, which I then sold for them. He was the Downer who'd taken over the neighbourhood.

"Thank you, Mr Holden, but we're fine," DI Milliner said.

"Are you arresting this man?" Holden asked. Around us, people had stopped laughing. Most of them stood and watched the Downer, though one or two of them began to head quietly to the doors.

"Yes, sir, we are. If you'd step aside, please?"

He ditched his cigarette and grinned at her, his cheeks cracking open, briefly revealing a molten interior before scabbing over quickly. The heat around us intensified as other Downers, three more of them, appeared, each one standing beside the DI's back-up men.

"Sir, I'd advise you — ", Milliner began.

"You're not taking him," Holden stated simply.

He reached out, his blackened hand grasping Milliner's throat. As she gagged, one of the other cops moved forward. Around us, the other Downers moved faster. Punches were thrown, but where they connected, the Downers' hands burned through clothes and flesh, plunging into the cops. People screamed, police and punters, and a mad rush to the doors began. The smell of burning skin soon replaced that of stale beer and wine; smoke heavy with human fat mingled with that of cigarettes as the Downers turned up their heat and butchered the policemen.

Right in front of me, the DI's head burst into flame, her hair going up in one brilliant, acrid-smelling flash as she screamed. From somewhere in her brain, her training or instincts reared up and she punched out at Holden, fingers taut and rigid, tearing into his throat. His neck erupted; molten blood gushed out of the wound, rolling over her arm, like lava from a volcano.

With the cops down, the three Downers looked to their boss. He and Milliner had both dropped to their knees, life draining out of the pair of them. As they rushed to help him, I weighed up my options and ran like hell.

*

The cops weren't like the RAF; they couldn't do pretty much as they pleased. There were procedures to follow, forms to fill in, warrants to be issued and probably a whole bunch of other stuff. The upshot of all that was that police HQ had known who it was that Milliner had gone out to arrest that night.

With the near-riot that had resulted after the Downers had appeared, it wasn't long before other cops arrived. They found Milliner and her guys dead, and although it was obvious that Downers had done it (you can't disguise the wounds they cause), I was their only lead. I suppose an old-fashioned APB was put out on me or something. One way or another, I quickly found out that the police were after me in connection with not only selling heroin, but also with the multiple murders of police officers.

Worse still, the Downers wanted me as well. With the sort of heat they could bring down on my head, I figured the best thing to do was get the hell out of the country.

It was Jerry I went to first; he was never actually part of the drugs trade, but he dabbled in a couple of other things. He got me out of the cuffs first, then arranged for transport, first to the Continent, then to the States.

Three days after I'd watched a policewoman's head go up in flames, I was sitting in a cheap hotel in New York, wondering what I was going to do next.

*

I didn't tell Corben any of that stuff. That's just a way of illustrating that God or the Devil quite often stick their heads out of the machine at some very opportune times. Which is exactly what happened after I'd finished telling Corben what I had really been planning.

Chapter Nine

Corben sat back in her chair and stared at me, a mixture of amazement and pity on her face. The can that she had been drinking from was still in her hand, though she hadn't moved it since I'd started talking, and behind me I could hear the steady breathing of the two guards; it was that quiet. Rhea was still unconcious and lay against the table, oblivious to everything; I didn't know if she had heard anything of what I'd said. Finally, Corben uncrossed her legs and winced as the pins and needles that had built up in her calf muscle began sewing beneath her skin.

"Christ Almighty, McKean," she said, leaning over and rubbing at her leg with one hand. "How the hell were you going to do that?"

I shrugged, too miserable and beaten to even answer. I didn't care anymore. I'd screwed the whole thing up, and too many people, friends of mine and others, had ended up dead or maimed for me to wonder anymore about how I was supposed to accomplish this stupid mission.

Corben looked up as someone unexpectedly knocked on the cell door. She nodded to one of the guards, who turned and stepped over to it. The door creaked as he opened it, there was the dull *phut!* of a silencer and suddenly clumps of bone and skin with hair still attached smacked into the back of my head and landed in my lap as a spray of fine red mist settled all around me.

The second guard turned, the silenced gun fired once again and this time, as I turned, I saw the guard's head exit out the rear of his helmet: a gout of blood followed by the back of his skull splintering through the ruptured metal. As both men fell to the ground, their killer stepped in front of me, his pistol pointed at Corben.

"Who the fuck are you?" she yelled as she tried to stand up, wobbling unsteadily as her sleepy leg almost spilled her to the floor.

I looked up at the killer, and I mean *up*. He was about six-and-a-half feet tall, and though he wore a long dark coat, hat and shades, where his arm poked out of his sleeve as he pointed his gun I could see the colourful edges of tattoos. As I realised who he was, I slowly tried to stand, to escape as quietly as I could. Without even looking at me, he reached over and grasped my shoulder, holding me in place.

Corben shook as the pistol pointed steadily at her head, the small black hole at its end oblivious to her indignant cries and pleas. The Tattooed Man smiled and shot her in the face.

Almost as an afterthought, the killer turned to where Rhea hung, still unconscious.

"No!" I cried, tugging on his arm. He faced me with that same smile he had given Corben and for a moment I expected him to shoot me, too.

"Why not?" he asked quietly, his cultured tones striking me as odd coming from a man, or an Upper at least, who had just mercilessly killed three people.

"Because she knows where the other half is," I said, lying frantically. "What I need to have, I only know where half of it is. She's got the location of the other piece."

The Tattooed Man stared at me for a moment, debating whether or not to believe me. Something on my face must have convinced him, or he didn't really care but wasn't taking any chances. Either way, he decided not to risk being wrong.

He let me go and stepped over to the desk, picking up Rhea's machete. With several quick, practised slices, he cut the bonds that held her, watching unconcerned as she slumped to the floor, her legs tangling in the sticky mess her bones and blood had made.

"Pick her up," he said to me, indicating her with the blade.

"I've got a broken leg," I whined, pointing down at the plaster cast that was still wrapped around me as if I were an unfinished Egyptian mummy. He sighed, weighing up the pros and cons of just shooting us both, then bent down and lifted Rhea easily, flinging her over his shoulder.

"You try and escape, and I'll kill her no matter what you say," he said, never once raising his voice. "Follow me. My car's outside."

*

"Outside" happened to be the rear of an RAF holding station in the back streets of God knows where. Over the last few years, as the Religious Armed Forces had grown to prominence, the stations had sprung up throughout not only the city, but also most of the country. They took over abandoned warehouses and renovated them, the work being done by an already sentenced and condemned workforce of rapists, child molesters and murderers. The general public had applauded their construction, cheering on the Godhead's pronouncements that the sick and wanton should give something back to the community that they had attacked before being justly executed. When the supply of convicted criminals ran out, however, there was still a need for more stations, and many of those who had previously cheered, primarily the unemployed, found themselves taking their places — not as people waiting to die, but more as residents taking part in an enforced community programme. As more stations were built, fewer people cheered for fear of being heard and made to join the site workers.

The three of us exited the building — me hobbling along on my bad leg, the Tattooed Man beginning to puff under the weight of Rhea — and stepped into what could have been, and at one time probably was, a coal yard. As in the scrubland outside the city where I'd met Rhea, old train tracks criss-crossed the ground, the brown and rusted remains of giant snail trails. There were roughly circular patches over to one side that were predominately black, all that was left of the huge piles of coal that had once been tipped there. Occasional lumps of coal still dotted the ground, sparkling in the fine drizzle that fell, looking like the stillborn corpses of diamonds. Oil, too, had left its mark over the expanse of grey concrete, mixing with the rain to create flawed and deformed rainbows.

Along one side of the yard, in the direction the Tattooed Man headed, were parked perhaps fifteen different cars and a couple of vans, the latter reminding me of the crazy car chase we'd gone through after leaving Hal's house all those weeks ago. Tears, brought on by the memory of Hal and the pain in my leg, threatened to spill down my face and join with the almost sticky drizzle that clung to me.

"Where are we going?" I called, looking back over my shoulder at the large building we had just come from. Windows peered through the rain at us, but if they were eyes in a face, they were blind. No one stood at any of them; the entire station gave the impression of being empty, lifeless. "How comes no one's following us?"

"I made sure we wouldn't be bothered," the Tattooed Man called back to me. Despite the weight of Rhea, his long legs had allowed him to pull away from me with my own stunted stride. If I were to catch up to him, my questions would have to wait.

He stooped to unlock a car that sat beside one of the RAF vans. I wondered if all Uppers owned them as I realised it was almost identical to the one that the Pale Man had picked me up in, after I'd phoned Roller way back when. Its windows were completely black, just like those on the other car and, as I stepped around to the rear passenger door and slipped inside, I noticed there was no handle on the interior.

The Tattooed Man opened the other back door and bundled Rhea inside, unmindful of how she landed. She was still out of it, and I arranged her in a sitting position as he closed the door and walked around to the driver's side. Shut in the pitch blackness, I had a moment of panic, unable to see him outside, unable even to see Rhea who sat less than two feet away from me. A second later, the Tattooed Man slid in to the driver's seat and turned on the interior light so that we could at least see each other, if not look out of the windows.

"Why didn't anyone stop us leaving?" I asked again, shuddering at the smile that greeted me in the rear-view mirror. I let the question lie and asked the next obvious one. "Where are we going now?"

The Tattooed Man chuckled. "Home, James," he said, starting the car and reversing out of the parking space. He turned the car around and drove off.

*

The ride through the streets of London took maybe an hour or so, although it was hard to judge the time for most of it because I couldn't see where we were going, wasn't wearing a watch and the Tattooed Man was hardly the most engaging of conversationalists. At some point Rhea moaned on the seat next to me, her eyelids fluttering. As I looked over at her I cursed myself and the Upper who had, technically at least, rescued us, because Rhea still wore the large strip of masking tape across her mouth.

Wincing in sympathy with her half-awake groan, I pulled the tape from her mouth as gently as I could, stroking her face and murmuring unintelligible sounds of comfort as she slowly came round. Having been unconscious myself a couple of times, I could guess roughly what she was going through; sounds generally came back first, at least for me they do, just snippets of either a nearby conversation, or the noise of a car engine; then you become aware of your limbs and how painfully heavy they are. You try moving them, but there's no co-ordination, no intelligent messages getting down to them; they flop about vaguely, new-born kittens trying to stand only to collapse to the floor. Your throat and mouth works next as you either try to talk or swallow, usually both at the same time. If, like Rhea, your mouth had been taped shut it's not so bad; it's worse if you're unconscious with your mouth wide open because you breathe through it, drying it and your throat out so that when you do surface, you feel as if your tongue has been placed inside a dry, crusty sock that doesn't smell too good either. Finally, as your brain decides that it would rather be back in the land of the living, or at least the fully aware, your eyesight returns, tunnel vision in reverse, as more and more light persuades your irises to let it in.

Very slowly, over the course of several minutes, I'd guess, Rhea went through all of this, her head rolling with the motion of the car, until she looked at me, her eyes struggling to stay more than half open.

"Aitch?" she whispered.

I glanced down at the bloodied and crusted remains of her hand which, even now when not entirely awake, she still cradled in her lap, trying to keep it from being knocked around. I remembered the look in her eyes as Corben had started to question me, and then sliced off Rhea's first finger joint, the gaze that said I was a dead man. I forced myself to look into the sleepy, half open eyes and prepared myself for the worse.

"I love you," she said quietly, smiled and fell asleep.

The rest of the drive, as I said, took place in silence.

*

"Mr McKean, I'm so pleased we finally get a chance to meet." Slake said as I entered the room. "I'd offer to shake hands, but . . . " The large Downer shrugged, a self-effacing grin cracking the skin around his mouth.

"That's okay. I can think of better ways to get blisters on my hand." I said, surprising myself. I sat down in the plush armchair, my leg sticking awkwardly out in front of me. I looked, smelled and felt clean for the first time in what seemed months. Sometime after leaving the holding station, the Tattooed Man had pulled the car into the courtyard of what turned out to be an old government owned building that had been sold to some millionaire or other several years ago. When that man had died, the present owner had acquired it and, to his credit, had left it much the same as it had been. He'd added bits and pieces of furniture, but for a Downer to leave something as beautiful as the interior of this house alone was frankly incredible; most Downer homes I'd been to were little more than hovels, permanently scorched and smoky from the heat of their inhabitants. Slake, however, revelled in the opulence of the place and even went so far as to deliberately not sit on any of the period piece furniture to avoid burning or marking it. He was obviously a Downer with a sense of taste and culture. I didn't trust him for a second.

Rhea sat in another armchair to my left, the three of us forming a triangle. She too looked a lot better than she had recently, though her eyes were still shadowed by dark smudges, the physical remnants of the shock she had suffered. Her hand was bandaged neatly and her arm was held by a loose sling. When we'd arrived at the mansion, we'd been separated and guided, by normal people I was glad to notice, to first bathrooms and then bedrooms. We'd washed and been given new clothes which, while they didn't fit exactly on me, weren't bad.

Before I pulled on the loose jeans I had been offered, the man-servant or guide or whatever the hell he was, had taken a small but sharp knife and sliced open the cast that was stuck like a snail shell to my leg. I'd protested but the man merely said, "Mr Slake's orders," and would not take no for an answer. Once I was dressed, the man left, locking me in the bedroom leaving me in no doubt about my "guest" status here. He returned soon after, though, with a large meal arranged on a tray, complete with both coffee and orange juice and it was with a grateful heart that I ate and drank my fill. I had to amuse myself in the room for another hour or so, flicking through the few books that were laying around, until he came back again, this time taking me downstairs. He handed me a walking stick and I made my way very carefully along the tiled floor which led to a large state room where Rhea and the Downer were already waiting for me.

Rhea avoided my gaze whenever I turned to look at her, but out the corner of my eye I could see her sneaking glances at me. The expression her face bore was not one I could work out, but I guessed she was either pissed off at me for putting her through the torture she'd suffered at Corben's hands, or she was regretting what she'd said in the car and was angry at herself.

To be honest, I had no idea whether she knew what she'd said in that brief moment of vague lucidity. She may not have even been seeing me; the shock and trauma may have confused her mind so that she professed her love to the wrong person. I had no idea. Either way, though, she was annoyed at something.

"You've led us a merry chase, Mr McKean," Slake said as he sat behind his desk, again a very modern piece of furniture like the chair he sat in. He was the first Downer I'd ever met who wasn't dressed in a basic suit and tie: he wore a T-shirt which had, of all things, an old faded print of Jim Morrison on the front, a cigarette dangling from his lips. With the constant smouldering of his body sending steam into the air, it seemed as if Morrison was actually smoking the damn thing. His arms, as black, crisp and cracked as the rest of his skin, bulged beneath the tight sleeves and I wondered if Downers worked out. His jeans, too, were tight against his thick legs, but not in the same way Corben's had been; there was muscle here, or whatever he had that passed for muscle. Poking out from under the desk as he leaned back in the chair were his feet, a pair of Jesus sandals slipped over them. Another reason I distrusted him.

"I was unaware you were after me," I said, bringing my gaze up to face him. No-one else was in the room, but I had no doubt that others were watching and listening somewhere. Whoever this guy was, and he was obviously important somewhere along the line, he wouldn't be left unguarded, not that Rhea or myself were in any state to cause him a problem.

"Oh come now, Mr McKean," Slake said with a chuckle, lava bubbling in his throat. "You must be aware that just about everybody who is anybody is aware, if not of *what* you profess to be carrying, then of the fact that you are carrying something *very* important. Things would have been a lot simpler if you'd gone with my compatriots that evening at the public house."

"What evening?" I asked, remembering a second later the night I'd been out with Jerry, the night he'd been killed. That was when I'd first encountered the Tattooed Man, Roller, and the Pale Man, the night this madness had started. "Oh," I said, "that evening,"

"Yes, that evening. You see, if you had gone with them they would have brought you here a long time ago. They did go to your friend's house later, but again you refused to join them. I can understand that we Downers aren't the best looking people in the world, but that hardly warrants cutting an arm off one of us,"

"Your man didn't exactly make it clear he meant no harm," I said. "And how do you fit in with Roller and the Pale Man, the Upper?"

"Roller is his own man," Slake said. "He has no interest, as far as I know, in whatever it is that you're carrying. The Pale Man, however — " he chuckled at my nickname for the Upper, " — I believe he's very interested. Isn't he, Miss Leary?"

We both looked at Rhea who glared back.

"How the hell should I know?" she said.

"You've worked for Straw, haven't you?" Slake asked with a grin.

"I've worked for you, as well. I've worked for lots of people. That's the whole point of being freelance,"

"Hang on. Who the hell is Straw?" I asked.

"The Pale Man, Mr McKean. Both Uppers and Downers do have names, you know. So, Miss Leary, what did Mr McKean employ you for? Something to do with his cargo?"

"Aitch hired me to help get him back to London after he'd been picked up by some gangster. Along the way I kinda lost a few digits," She held up her hand, or the remains of it, and stared over at me. It seemed pretty obvious that it was me she blamed. "I don't know what he's got and I don't care. I just want to go home. I've had enough of this bullshit."

Slake nodded. "I can understand that, Miss Leary. We would like you, however, to remain as our guest for just a little longer while we sort some things out with Mr McKean. Is that amenable?"

"Do I have a choice?"

The Downer's smile faded and spread his hands apologetically. "I'm afraid not." He turned back to me, his lips peeling back slowly revealing his teeth again, flirtatious oysters showing their wares. "Would you like tell us exactly what it is you're carrying around in your rucksack, Mr McKean, and what you intend to do with it?"

For the first time since I'd woken in the hospital, I found myself itching for a cigarette. However long it was I'd spent in that bed had managed to clean all the nicotine out of my system, the physical addiction, but now the habit of smoking when I was stressed, the psychological side, reached out to me, tempting me with its smoky siren call.

"I don't have it," I said simply, trying not to bite my fingernails when I stroked the stubble that now graced my chin. "I don't know where it is,"

"Could you have left it in the holding station, perhaps?" Slake asked, his smile never wavering. As I looked at that smug little grin, I knew he was toying with me. "Or could

Page have found it before he picked you up?"

"Page?" I asked, completely thrown off track.

"The Upper with the tattoos, the one who saved you." So the Tattooed Man finally had a name as well, I thought. "You see, Mr McKean, you were a secondary target. I sent Page into that station to get, first and foremost, your rucksack. If he could find you in time, then I asked him to bring you along as well. From what he has told me, you convinced him enough that Miss Leary here had something to do with your mad little scheme that he brought her along too." Slake's smiled faltered slightly, the black pits of his eyes narrowing slightly as he reached down beside him and lifted, of all things, the battered old rucksack that I'd taken with me when I'd had to leave the country all those years ago.

"I've had people examining this thing all afternoon," Slake said. He turned it round and round on its strap, twirling it. The pockets all hung loose; the straps had had their stitching undone; the zips were now toothless. Twisting on his finger, it resembled nothing more than a gutted fish hanging from a hook. "They have found absolutely nothing out of the ordinary at all," With a flick of his wrist he turned the bag upside down, his arm now inside it, and began rolling it around his forearm, staring at me all the while. "Some clothes, a book or two, a bunch of keys and sundry toiletries. There is nothing of any sort of value in this thing at all, McKean," he said tightly, the first crack in his pretence of charm and sophistication. The bag revolved around his arm faster and faster, the heat building inside as he concentrated, raising the temperature until, inevitably, the rucksack burst into flames. Slake continued swinging it as it burned, the flames trailing behind the bag until it began to disintegrate, charred and blackened pieces drifting away, mingling with the thick smoke that hung heavy against the ceiling. Finally, as he stopped its movement, the remains hung limp and crisp from his hand, a few meagre licks of yellow trying to find more fuel but dying out, starved to death.

With a noticeable effort, Slake calmed himself, his smile breaking through the ravages of his face once more as what was left of my bag fell from his arm. He shifted position slightly and stamped on the smouldering cloth.

"There never was anything in there, was there McKean? I don't really count the outdated information on the computer disc that we also retrieved from the station; you could have done no real damage with that and I don't think you'd go to all this trouble for something as trivial as that."

Rhea stared at me, a frown on her face. She was confused, wondering why I'd been so insistent on getting the rucksack if there was nothing in it. I ignored her and looked back at Slake's hungry face.

"What if you're wrong, Slake? What if I really am that small and petty-minded to think the information on that disc was worth everything I've been through? I never started out to do anything except pass on a few embarrassing details about the dear old Godhead in the hope that people would get off their fat arses and do something. Everything else has just exploded around me. My friend got killed; I got implicated; I went for help to some dubious guys; next thing I know, the RAF, the gangsters and you guys are all after me. I thought you were all after the disc, but you've all said it's worthless. I don't have anything else. If you're expecting some big revelation about some secret I've got tucked away somewhere, you're in for a long wait because it doesn't exist.

"This whole thing's just got out of hand. I had my disc. I wanted to spread some news. That's it."

Out of the corner of my eye, I saw Rhea stand quickly. Before I could react she was on me, beating at me with her left hand, her nails scratching at my face, pulling my hair as she yelled at me.

"I lost my hand for fuck all? You bastard! You piece of fucking shit!"

She slipped off me and for a second I thought she'd given up. That was when she kicked my recently broken leg with as much force as she could. I screamed, clutching at my leg just as she kicked it again, hurling obscenities at me, our cries joining together with the rasping laughter of the Downer. I reached out and grabbed her foot as she took another swing and pushed her back, toppling her on to the floor, my tears of pain blurring the sight of her landing on her back.

"Please, enough," Slake said still laughing. Rhea and I looked at him, she picking herself up, me holding the throbbing ball of agony that was my leg. "Enough, enough," His chuckles died down and he sighed, looking at us both with the air of an indulgent father who had found his spoilt children squabbling. "You could have saved yourself that pain if you'd told me the truth, Mr McKean," he said. "I know you have something other than that worthless disc and the old and useless information it contains." He leaned forward on his desk. "I'd just like to know what."

Rhea stood carefully, instinctively using her right hand to pull herself up on the chair, crying out at the pain it caused her. As she got to her feet, she stared at me, her face hard and set.

"Tell him the truth, Aitch," she said quietly. I noticed her left hand was clenched tightly, her knuckles white as if angry themselves, mourning the loss of their sisters. "There has to be more than that disc. If you made me go through everything that Corben did to me for nothing . . . I swear I'll kill you."

Slake looked over at me, the crisp, dark pork scratching face cracking once more as he smiled at me, his eyes open and expectant.

I was a cat's whisker away from telling the truth, telling them everything that had so shocked Corben when something that Rhea said lodged in my mind, a verbal squatter refusing admittance to anything else. I almost asked her, curiosity grappling with the despair that crept over me again, the same depression that made me blurt everything to Corben.

I had to stop and think. I closed my eyes, ridding myself of the fevered looks they were both giving me and racked my memory, hoping I was wrong. I wasn't convinced that my sudden suspicion was correct, that I wasn't just being paranoid . . . but I couldn't convince myself I was wrong, either. But if I was right, that threw everything that I knew, everything that I'd experienced into complete confusion. I needed time to think, time to sort things through. The only thing I could do was stall them with half-truths.

I opened my eyes and looked at them.

"This entire thing, the reason so many people have been after me, it's all been based on a lie. Several lies, I should say. The disc contains information about the lack of births over the last God knows how many years, that much is true. As you and so many others have told me, the data is old and practically useless. However, it's the only thing I have.

"I came back into the country only a few weeks ago. I was met by my friend, Jerry. He was the one involved with a group that wants to get rid of not only the Godhead, but also every other Upper or Downer. I don't know anybody else in the organisation. Jerry arranged a meeting for us near the Houses of Parliament. There's a pub round there, the Mason's Arms, which some MPs drink in. We were meant to be in the bar every evening at seven o'clock until someone contacted us. I had to give them the disc and that was it: my part was done. I knew no names, didn't know who I was expecting or when he or she was due to turn up. I was just a courier," I sighed, and found myself wanting a cigarette again. "If Jerry hadn't been killed that night after we left the pub, if another friend hadn't already introduced me to the guy called Roller, I might not be here and all this bollocks wouldn't have happened."

I glanced over at Rhea, my most sincere look on my face. "I'm sorry," I said quietly.

Slake sat back in his chair, his arms crossed, his biceps bulging under the T-shirt, the sleeves of which were looking a little crisp and blackened. He stared at me, trying to make up his mind whether to believe me or not.

"And that, I take it, is the truth?" he said after a moment. I nodded. "You've watched a friend lose the fingers of her hand, knuckle by knuckle from what she's told me, and you held out just to prevent the RAF from discovering that, by your own admission, you're nothing more than a courier, a delivery boy. Give me one reason why I should believe you."

He reached into a drawer and pulled out a pistol, aiming it casually at me.

"One reason, Mr McKean,"

Christ knows how I did it, but I managed to ignore the gun and stare directly at Slake. With a grin and a half chuckle, I simply said "Because it's the truth," and shrugged, hoping it was the best "see if I give a damn" shrug I'd ever performed.

Slake stared at me, the pistol never wavering from its aim. My feet wanted to tap; my fingers were itching to wrap around themselves, strangling each other; my whole body wanted to perform its own nervous St Vitus dance as I waited for Slake to weigh up what I'd said. I managed to keep still, my eyes never dropping from his own gaze, my embarrassed, self-effacing half smile striving to look natural.

With a laugh of his own, Slake replaced the pistol in the drawer, still watching me, waiting for any sign that I was relaxing now that the danger was apparently over. When I did nothing, just sat there calmly looking at him, he finally closed the drawer.

"You really are a pathetic specimen, McKean," he said with a laugh. Beside me, Rhea said nothing. "Well, if you were due to meet somebody in the Mason's Arms, we'd better make sure you get there." He looked over to the other side of the room where an ornate and probably antique grandfather clock sat, which judging by the size of it must have been several more greats removed from your average grandfather, gently ticking away the hours and minutes. "It's too late to get you there now, but tomorrow we shall arrange to have you driven down to this pub so that you can see if your little contact shows. And we shall make sure you're there until your contact shows, however long it may take. After all, this mysterious group of rebels might need some help in bringing down the government . . . and I so want to help, as I'm sure you do."

Slake leaned across the table, his smile tearing open his cheeks again, tiny drops of bright red liquid dribbling down his face until they hardened like stalactites from his chin.

"Don't you, McKean?"

Chapter Ten

Rhea didn't talk to me the next day, even though Slake allowed us the run of the house. We had breakfast together and, though we explored the place separately, we'd occasionally bump into each other in a room or a corridor, but she still wouldn't say anything. I found myself wondering about my suspicions, asking myself if I was being too paranoid, but I couldn't ask her outright just in case I was right. After our lunch, as I sat alone in my room, I stared out of the window, racking my brains, trying desperately to find a memory that would prove me wrong.

The day before, after Rhea had kicked and punched me, she'd stood up and told me that if she'd gone through everything that Corben had put her through for nothing, then she'd kill me.

She mentioned Corben by name.

When Corben had interrogated me first in my own cell, she told me she had yet to see Rhea. As far as I could remember, when the RAF officer had been torturing Rhea, her name had never been mentioned, and Rhea had been unconscious for most of the time before the Tattooed Man, Page, had rescued us.

How did Rhea know Corben's name? What did it mean?

A knock at the door heralded the arrival of Slake's man-servant and the end of my musings.

"If you're ready, Mr McKean, the master of the house will see you now."

*

"Mr McKean, all ready for your journey I presume?"

"Journey?"

Slake grinned and puffed on a cigarette. "But of course. As I said yesterday, you are going to fulfil your capacity of courier. On the table you will find your precious computer disc. Oh, don't worry: it hasn't been tampered with in anyway. All the information on there is as it was. Completely out dated and useless, as I keep telling you, but if your friends want it, they can have it." He waved his hand in the direction of the table where the disc sat along with the keys that had been in the rucksack. I picked the disc up and slipped it into the pocket of the jacket I'd been given, and the keys into my jeans. I turned at the sound of heavy boots coming down the corridor and was surprised to see Rhea, once more wearing her jeans, long black coat and wide brimmed hat. I couldn't see it, but I was willing to bet she had her machete strapped to her leg again as well.

"Ah, my dear, leaving so soon?" Slake said. She ignored him for a moment, staring over at me.

"I've had enough of this bullshit," she said eventually. "I don't give a toss what he's trying to do with whatever information he's got. I just want to get home."

Slake chuckled, tapping ash into a porcelain ashtray.

"You must do as you see fit, Miss Leary. However, I would caution you against seeking revenge on Mr McKean, here. He's now under my protection and, while I can fully understand your grievance with him, I would ask that your put your rage on hold for a few days, at least,"

"I'll see you soon, Aitch," Rhea said, ignoring Slake's little speech. I couldn't look at her for more than a second or two before I dropped my gaze. She turned and headed for the door.

"You've made yourself an enemy there, Mr McKean," Slake said to me after she had gone. "Not a very smart move,"

"What do you want me to do?" I asked him quietly.

"Exactly what you originally set out to do," Slake said, taking my arm and steering me towards the door. The heat from his hand filtered through the jacket sleeve quickly and I was glad when he let go to hold the door for me. On the drive outside sat the black, tinted windowed car that had brought me here and, leaning against the bonnet, was Page, the Tattooed Man.

"I want you to go to the Mason's Arms," Slake said, "and meet up with this mysterious MP of yours, if MP he is. Chat with him, give him the disc, let him go on his way. Then, once that's done, we'll see about letting you go on yours."

"What if he doesn't turn up tonight?" I asked. Slake

shrugged, unconcerned.

"Then tomorrow night we take you down there again. You'll sit for a maximum of three hours each night until your contact approaches you. Page will, of course, be watching you, to make sure you don't flee. You'll only have a small amount of money," Slake handed me a crisp twenty pound note, "so you won't be getting drunk, but by all means try and enjoy yourself." He laughed again and half patted me on the back, half shoved me towards the car, sending me hobbling with my walking stick.

Page grinned as he opened the back door for me, slamming it shut once I was in. A moment later he started the car and, in total darkness, drove me back into London.

*

"Not often we get a new face in here," the barman said as he placed my pint on the bar in front of me. It was the most anyone had said to me since I'd arrived and now, as the end of my three hours was fast approaching it seemed that was the most I was going to get. Looking around the interior of the Mason's Arms was depressing to say the least; the actual building was okay — lots of wooden beams and fine old paintings depicting country scenes, with a real fake coal fire tucked away in one corner. The people who were drinking and talking around me, though . . . it wasn't until I was sat in a nest of obviously affluent people that I realised just how envious I was of them and their wealth. I didn't see a bunch of guys in shirts and ties out having a drink after work; with my inbred, bigoted and blinkered view I saw half a dozen suits, laughing about how they'd shafted the poor people again. They were the ones who'd had everything handed to them on a plate; they hadn't had to work to get where they were because they and, undoubtedly, their families were rich; the world had offered up everything they'd ever need free and for nothing. They had no money worries; they didn't need to wonder if they could pay the rent or feed their families; they had no conception of how things were in the "real world"; they were wilfully blind and ignorant of the troubles and concerns of the little men.

I stared at them over my pint and realised what bollocks

I was thinking. I knew nothing about these people; I was merely taking stereotypes and generalisations and applying them across the board. With a sigh, I turned back to the barman.

"Sorry, what did you say?"

"I said it's not often we get a new face in here." He nodded at my jeans and jacket. "It's obvious you don't work in the Houses. What brings you in here?"

The barman stood in his tight red waistcoat, the front bulging slightly around his middle-aged spread, the lights of the bar shining through the thinning hair on top of his head. As he talked, he wiped one wine glass after another, quick practised motions that spoke volumes about how long he'd been doing it.

"I'm supposed to be meeting someone in here," I said, too bored, tired and depressed to offer any more.

"Girl trouble, eh mate?" he asked with a laugh. "Ah, it's alright, she'll turn up sooner or later,"

"You think so?"

"Nah, not really." He finished with the last wine glass and set them all hanging from the racks above the bar, their bowls pointing downward to catch the least amount of dust and the maximum amount of cigarette smoke. "No offence mate, but you've been sat there for what, two an' half, three hours. No one's spoken to you, no-one's even bothered you for a light, you obviously don't know anybody and therefore, with my wonderful sense of deduction, I reckon you've been stood up." He laughed again.

"Thanks," I said dryly. A smug barman was all I needed. As I sat there, though, I realised that wasn't exactly true. I asked him where the toilets were and, armed with directions, made my way to the gents. Page stood in a corner by the door, his height, colour and brooding silence kept everyone away from him, which gave him an uninterrupted view of me. As far as I knew, he hadn't had a single drink all evening. He watched me head into the toilets, but didn't follow. I wondered why for a second before I noticed the only other way out of there was through a rotary fan tucked high into the corner of the sterile looking room. No windows, just a fan. Page knew

I wasn't going anywhere.

I stepped up to the urinal and let nature take over. The door opened and another man walked in, dressed in a suit and tie like all the others. For a second I wondered if he was my contact, but judging from the look of disdain that hung on his face, I guessed not. I looked away and stared down at the trough where wet, brown cigar butts lay like children's turds being washed down the drain.

I finished up and returned to my seat at the end of the bar, slowly drinking my pint. After serving someone else, the barman walked back over to me.

"Listen, sorry mate,"

"About what?" I asked.

"That stuff about being stood up. It's not fun; Christ knows I should know that," He looked at me then offered his hand. "Me name's Brian, Bri to me mates,"

I smiled, thankful at least for the offer of some sort of friendship. "Aitch, like the letter," I said, instantly thinking the line made me sound like a dick. Brian didn't flinch though.

"If you want, I can keep an eye out for her. I mean, that's unless you're going to be here all night," I shook my head and glanced over at Page who was frowning at me.

"No, it's okay, thanks. Sorry to ruin your detective work, but I haven't actually been stood up." Brian raised an eyebrow. "I'm supposed to be meeting someone, that's all. Gotta pass something on,"

He stood suddenly, both hands on the top of the bar. "If it's drugs you can fuck off right now," he said quietly so no-one else would hear.

"No, it's not drugs. Someone's supposed to be meeting me, like I said. It's all fairly kosher," After a moment he relaxed and folded his arms, leaning on the bar. I glanced at the clock over the fake fire and saw I had less than five minutes. I downed the last of my beer and placed the glass in front of him. "Listen, you gonna be serving tomorrow night?"

"Far as I know," he said.

"Okay, if anyone comes in looking for Aitch McKean, unless it's the police," I added in a stage whisper, "tell them

I'll be back in here tomorrow at seven. That okay?"

"Yeah, no worries,"

I stood and did my jacket back up, thanked him and headed out the door, Page stepping out after me. "Before you ask me, that was the barman. He thought I'd been stood up by a girl and was just trying to be friendly,"

"I know," Page said, taking a tiny receiver out of his ear. As we stood at the kerb, Page unlocking the door, I scanned my jacket, pulling out the pockets and turning up the lapels until, stuck to the collar, I found a small black dot which could only be a microphone. Page smiled at me and held the door open. "We want to make sure we know when you get your contact, McKean," he said.

"How the hell do you drive these things, anyway?" I asked suddenly, dutch courage running through my veins. "I mean, I can't see a bloody thing,"

Page took a pair of shades out of his pocket and, after a second's thought, handed them to me. I slipped them on and looked at the car. The windows were completely clear and almost looked to be illuminated; everything in the car was visible, but the view turned black instantly as Page took the glasses off me.

"How does that work?" I asked.

"You don't need to know," he said.

As I stepped into the car, Big Ben struck ten and it began to snow, the light flakes drifting to the ground to die beneath the wheels of the car as it moved off.

*

Over the next couple of days, Slake was nowhere to be found. Whenever I approached one of his aides I would be told that he was in the city "on business". No matter how genial I tried to be, though, I couldn't get through their hard outer shell of polite formality; they weren't going to tell me who Slake was or what business he was about. My sole purpose, the only reason Slake let me live, was to deliver the disc so that they, whoever "they" really were, could find my contact and from him or her, track down any dissenting voices against the Godhead. At least, that's what I was guessing.

Each evening, Page would appear and drive me down to the Mason's Arms where I would sit at the corner of the bar and, if Brian was serving, have a chat. He only worked four nights a week, meaning that for some of that first week I spent a lonely three hours sat on my own, trying to make my beer last, fighting against the still persistent urge for a cigarette. As the days wore on, a few of the regulars began nodding at me as they stood at the bar. They didn't engage me in conversation, but they were beginning to recognise my presence, something which, on the first night I'd been there, I was sure they'd never do.

Finally, at the start of my second week of being a part-time barfly, someone other than Brian actually spoke to me.

"You got a light, mate?"

I looked up from my beer at the young suit in front of me. Very professional, very neat and tidy, the only thing that let him down was his tie having been loosened at the neck, his collar undone after a hard days graft. He held up a cigarette and stared at me with his dark blue eyes. For a second I wondered if this was some sort of code; should I reply that I never carry a light when the moon is in its second phase and the owl is hooting twice or some such bollocks? That's what drinking alone does for you. Instead, I shook my head.

"Sorry, I quit a while back,"

His eyes widened in what seemed to be genuine surprise. "Jesus, how'd you do it?"

"I had a car crash. Spend about three or four weeks in a hospital bed completely unconscious and you kinda lose the habit," I said with a smile.

"Well, it's obviously worked, but I'd say that's just a bit extreme for my liking. I prefer the tried and tested way where you go out for a beer, smoke about forty fags in one night and swear you'll never do it again when you wake up the next morning with enough tar in your lungs to cover the M25." He chuckled slightly. "Then of course you go out the next evening and you say, well I'll just have a couple. Trouble is, it's usually a couple of packets again,"

He stuck his unlit cigarette into the corner of his mouth and held out his hand.

"Kyle Parobeck," I took his hand and shook it.

"Aitch McKean,"

As Kyle began to talk again, hunting around on the bar for a discarded book of matches, I glanced over at Page who still stood alone in his corner. He wasn't looking at me, but his face was adorned with a little smile that told me he was listening to everything we said.

*

At lunch time the following day, I was called into the same room where Slake had 'interviewed' Rhea and I. He sat at his desk again, this time wearing jogging bottoms and a sweatshirt, and indicated the seat opposite. Beside it, on a small stool, was a light lunch; salad, a few cold meats; fresh bread rolls with butter; a small pot of tea. I sat down and began to help myself. It was hardly the most traditional meal for the time of year — it would be Christmas all too soon — but it was nice enough.

"This Kyle Parobeck character," Slake said as I ate, without looking up from the papers he was reading. I noticed he was very careful not to touch them for too long in case he scorched them. "Ever met him before? Heard his name? Seen his face?"

"No to all three," I said honestly enough. Kyle had talked with me for most of the evening until I'd left, as arranged, at ten. From what he'd said, he worked in the Houses of Parliament but he didn't say what as. He'd appeared to be a friendly enough guy, someone who just happened to ask for a light and get a conversation in return, and I told Slake as much.

"Yes, yes, I've heard the tape of your little tête-à-tête. I'm sure he's a very lovely man. Do you think he's your contact?"

I shrugged. "I don't know. On the outside, he just seems like a nice guy who'll chat to anyone. I suppose he could be the guy I'm waiting for," Slake glanced up, studied my face for a moment, then turned back to his papers. He seemed to be concentrating and, as loudly as I could, I crunched on a fresh stick of celery. God knows how he managed to have celery in December, but it was worth chewing the hideous stuff just to see him frown at me.

"I want you to go to the Mason's Arms again tonight. See if this Parobeck person turns up. Talk with him, as you did last night. Don't mention the disc or the Godhead or any nonsense about rebellion. Let him start that particular ball rolling." He stared at me, his face serious. "But this is going on a little too long McKean. I want results within the week. Otherwise we might just have to close this whole thing down, and without the need for you to deliver the disc, there's no need for you. Understand?"

*

There used to be something comforting in going to a pub where you're regarded as a regular. You knew that even if you were sat on your own, sooner or later someone you knew, another regular, would come in and swap a few words with you. You could guarantee that there would be someone to talk to, someone you could have a laugh and a drink with as you wile away the hours till closing time. Sadly, in the Mason's Arms, I wasn't a regular. Sure, I'd been drinking there every night for the last week and a half, but it wasn't by choice, and the other people in there, the real regulars, those who worked in the Houses across the road, they could somehow sense that I was just a passing fad. They were the ones who came in most lunch times and afternoons, who knew that there would be some-one to talk to even if they walked in on their own. I was just someone who had taken to sitting at the bar by himself. They probably wondered where I'd come from and, when I stopped going there, they might wonder where I'd gone. But there would be no worry in their voices; if one of their own crowd disap-peared, just stopped turning up, they'd want to find out why. If I wasn't sat at the bar one night, they'd shrug their shoulders and carry on with their lives. There's nothing so lonely as a pub where no-one knows your name.

"Alright, Aitch?" Brian the barman said as I took my now usual seat. His greeting made me realise how maudlin my thoughts had become and I smiled and said hi. "Usual?" he asked, already pouring me a pint. I may never be a regular, I thought, but at least I could have a conversation here. He took my money and, as he handed me my change, said "Someone was in today asking for you,"

"Was it Kyle?" I asked. He stared at me for a moment then asked what Kyle looked like. I described him as best I could, mentioning his dark blue eyes. He shook his head slowly, frowning as he tugged on his ear.

"Might have been. Can't say I remember, really. Back in a second, okay?" I watched, confused, as Brian walked off.

The minutes dragged by as I sipped my pint, watching most of the faces that I'd come to know go through their usual display of the evening. There was the group of five or six young men who, every night, stood in the same corner and watched every woman in the place with a hungry look in their eyes and their tongues almost hanging out of their mouths; I'd never seen one of them approach any woman. Standing near the fire, a couple smiled and talked quietly with each other, the man staring up at the taller woman, the pair of them oblivious to anything other than each other; quite sickening, really. At the other end of the spectrum was another couple, slightly older, who stood together and looked at everything except each other; I couldn't help wondering if the first two would end up like them after all the glamour and romance had worn off — I surprised myself by hoping they didn't. A group of five women sat round a table getting through a steady stream of cocktails; laughing uproariously at just about anything one of them said; at about nine they'd leave and head off, presumably, to a night-club to dance the night away or get picked up. With a sigh born of drink and depression, I wished I could swap this ridiculous life I was leading for one of theirs.

"Hey, Aitch, how you doing?" Kyle said, suddenly appearing at my shoulder, drink in one hand, cigarette in the other.

"Not too bad," I said. "You?"

"Top of the world, mate. Had a bit of luck yesterday. One of my horses came in and I'm gonna pick up a nice little package," He grinned at me. For a second I couldn't work out what he was talking about, but as he winked at me the reference made sense. Since the Godhead's rule began, reforms had filtered in to the law, one of which was the banning of all gambling; horses didn't run anymore. I stared at Kyle, unable to say anything when Brian arrived back.

"Get you something?" he asked Kyle.

"No, I'm alright for now, thanks,"

"Sir?" he asked me, completely straight faced. Five minutes ago he'd greeted me by name, now he was calling me "sir"?

"No, no I've still got most of this," I said holding up my pint.

"Something to eat, sir? Crisps, nuts, a sandwich? The rolls are very good this evening, sir,"

This was too weird. I went with my instincts and ordered a roll. As Brian went to the other end of the bar, I turned back to Kyle.

"You couldn't do me a favour, could you?" I handed him a five pound note. "I've decided to start smoking again. You couldn't get me some from the fag machine, could you? My leg's playing me up," I added, lifting up my walking stick.

"Sure, no problem," he said after a moment's hesitation. "What do you smoke?"

"I don't mind. Anything other than Silk Cut,"

"Don't fancy toy fags, then, eh?"

As Kyle walked off to get my cigarettes, Brian returned with a roll on a paper plate, covered with cellophane, and a napkin beside it. He asked for the money and, as he turned to the till, flipped the napkin over. Written in small letters was HE'S RAF — ARE YOU WIRED? Brian brought my change back and, as he handed it over, pointed very casually to the question on the napkin.

"Well, sir? How is it?"

I made a pretence of picking up the roll, pointing at the napkin myself.

"Yes, yes. Very good," I desperately wanted to look over at Page to see if he was registering the formality of our conversation, but I didn't want to alert him to anything if he wasn't already. Brian took the napkin and balled it up, stuffing it in his pocket.

"I'll be back in a moment," he said, walking away as Kyle returned, my new cigarettes in hand, and sat down.

"Here you go. How's the roll?"

"Good," I said again.

"I didn't ask you last night what you do. How comes you started drinking here?"

I shrugged. "I was supposed to meet someone, hand something over to him." I grinned and tapped the side of my nose. "All very hush-hush, you know?"

He chuckled, glancing around before leaning in to me. "I'd say you've met someone, wouldn't you?" Dropping his voice to whisper he said "Aitch, if you've got it with you, we can leave now. My car's waiting outside."

I stared into his dark blue eyes as I chewed on a mouthful of ham roll. Swallowing, I took a sip of beer to wash it down with.

"Got what?" I asked.

His smile faltered a little. "You know," he said.

"My contact knew what I'd be carrying. You don't. Obviously you're not him,"

Kyle gritted his teeth and uttered a harsh "Fuck!" before pushing back the side of his jacket, revealing a pistol in a holster. "McKean, you come with me and you bring whatever it is you're supposed to be carrying,"

Brian appeared at the bar beside us, another roll balanced on his hand.

"I thought you might like one, too, sir," he said to Kyle. As he stood up and looked at Brian, I stole a glance at Page who was watching us intently, a grin on his face.

"What?" Kyle asked. Brian moved the plate to one side with his other hand. A small pistol, complete with silencer, was pointed at him. The plump barman smiled at him.

"No firearms allowed in this establishment, sir," he said loudly, "You should know that, being an RAF officer and all." At his words, just about everyone in the bar turned to look at Kyle, murmurs ran through the crowd. More than a couple of people picked up their coats and began to leave. "Please place your weapon on the bar, sir, the barrel facing in your direction. Mr McKean," Brian said, "Would you like to take the officer's pistol?" Kyle and Brian stared at each other as I carefully picked up the gun Kyle had placed on the bar, aiming it at the RAF man. "Now lift the partition and get behind the bar."

Throughout the bar, as quickly and quietly as possible, people were leaving, some not even bothering to stop and collect their coats or bags, casting worried glances at the three of us. Kyle sighed, a look of supreme boredom on his face. He tilted his head to the right and clearly said "Negative target acquisition." into his collar before he suddenly dropped to the floor. Brian stepped forward to look carefully over the bar as I turned to check on Page.

Page had moved out of the corner and was stood in front of the doors, shooting the bolts on both of them as people stopped in front of him, telling him to get out of the way. He stared over at me, his smile long gone. When he saw he had my attention, he pulled a pistol, the barrel looking absurdly huge, from inside his coat and grabbed one of the pub's customers at random, pointing the gun at his head. I saw him raise his eyebrow at me before one of the windows was smashed open, a steel canister landing on the floor.

"Shit!" Brian hissed, ignoring where Kyle had gone. Almost as if his exclamation had triggered it, the top of the canister exploded, filling the place instantly with grey smoke. Women were screaming as they headed for the door, men yelling and crying, pushing each other out of the way, looking for an exit other than that which the Upper that was blocking. "Go! Out the back!" Brian called to me, his hand over his mouth, trying not to inhale the smoke.

"McKean!" Page cried. I looked over in his direction, but the smoke was already too thick in that corner and all I could see were vague shapes blurring together as they tried to push past him to get through the still-locked doors. Then, smashing its way through the cries of the ordinary people who had just come for a pint after work, came the flat, dead sound of a pistol going off. The public were silenced for a second that seemed to last an hour before someone screamed that she was covered in blood, her cries ending in ragged coughs and retching. "Get over here, McKean, or I kill another one!" Page called.

Brian pushed me along the bar as I hesitated, herding me toward the door that led to the back of the pub while also frantically peering through the smoke, trying to see if Page had another hostage.

"McKean!" The shout came from the end of the bar and I whirled, pistol up and pointing at whomever had called. It was Kyle, still hunched behind the bar, and judging by the muffled quality of his voice, it seemed a good bet he was wearing a gas mask. "McKean! Give it up! We can protect you from the Downers!"

The pub window broke again, but this time it was the entire thing, frame and all, as a man wearing a gas mask and the matte black of the Church Police, crashed through and instantly fixed his rifle sights on me. Another followed, and still more, some pointing their guns at me and Brian, others over at the huddled, screaming and coughing mass at the door. Their laser sights darted thin red beams through the smoke.

"Surrender, McKean!" Kyle shouted.

"Go! Move!" Brian said, pushing me backwards to the door.

"McKean!" Page yelled.

The Upper threw his hostages out of the way and took the few steps to the bar as quickly as he could. The smoke was swept behind him, rolling around him as he charged through it, his face fixed with a look of rage as he dived towards me. I heard Brian swear quietly, and saw him trying to bring his pistol up as Page emerged from the billowing gloom, before there was a dull crack, the sound of a high-powered rifle, followed by another and another.

Page was thrown off his feet, twisting in the air as the bullets smacked into him, two into his chest, one into his head. Even before he fell, the whole thing looking like some bizarre, slow-motion ballet piece, light burst out from the wounds. From the entry and exit holes in his chest and back, beams of light streamed out, perfectly cylindrical, stabbing through the cloud of gas that coiled around him as he fell like stage lights illuminating his final performance. The top of his head almost erupted, his scalp ripping back above his eyes, sending shards of matter sprinkling over the wall behind him. Brilliant white light exploded from his skull, a searchlight gazing upwards but finding nothing other than the nicotine-stained ceiling.

With a last sigh, Page rolled to a halt next to the wall, and the lights from his body went out.

Brian took advantage of the lull in the activity; probably none of the public and maybe only a few of the Church Police had ever seen an Upper die before. Everyone had frozen; even the people who stood gathered in the smoke at the door did nothing more than cough slightly.

The barman pushed me and we moved through the door into the back room, dodging the crates of bottles, cans and crisps, wincing as we heard Kyle's muffled shout a moment later and the sound of breaking glass as members of the Church Police squad dived over the bar. We frantically scrabbled at the back door, pushing it closed behind us once we were through, throwing bottle crates around it in the hope of slowing any pursuers, then, with Brian wheezing and puffing and me limping and cursing, we dived into his car.

As we pulled out of the car park, the rear door of the pub opened and two riflemen ran headlong into the crates, spilling over each other as we hit the road.

"I take it you're my contact, then, Brian?" I said as I got my breath back, leaning down and massaging my leg.

"I am if you've got the merchandise," he said, speeding along the mainly deserted back streets until he came to a main junction, then slowing down and driving like any normal person.

"What merchandise?" I asked him, not liking the way he used that word. It conjured images of the drug deals in alleys which I'd left behind me many years ago.

"What do you think I mean?" he yelled, never taking his eyes off the road. Big Ben and the Houses of Parliament began to recede behind us as we drove further away from the Mason's Arms and the mess that had happened there. I turned and look out of the back window, expecting to see Church Police vans speeding after us, but there was only the late evening traffic. "Have you got it or not?"

"Got what?" I asked slowly. If he asked for the wrong thing, I didn't care what speed we were going at or that we were on a main road; I was diving out of the door, bad leg or not.

Brian sighed and brought his temper back under control. He reached into his waistband where he had stowed his pistol and, as I shrank back in my seat, nervously reaching for my own gun, he tossed it into the back seat.

"The Key, McKean," he said, slowing at a red light. "Have you got the Key?"

I almost fainted with relief. Finally, someone else knew what I was carrying.

"Yes," I said, closing my eyes and relaxing for what seemed like the first time since birth. "Yes, I have."

Chapter Eleven

"We're not out of the woods yet," Brian explained as he drove. "There's gonna be Church Police and RAF cameras watching out for our every move as soon as that son of a bitch Parobeck gets in touch with his bosses."

"What do we do?" I asked, scrabbling around the collar of my jacket until I found the small microphone. I pulled it off and tossed it out the window. The big barman shrugged.

"Lose 'em."

A few minutes later he pulled into a quiet street off the main drag and parked up as soon as he could. We got out of the car, Brian leaving his gun in the back seat and telling me to do the same. "We'll leave the engine running and the keys in the ignition," he said, taking his red waistcoat off and throwing that in as well. From the back seat he took a long overcoat, buttoning it against the dull, cold drizzle that seemed to float more than fall. "Hopefully someone'll steal it soon. It won't throw them for long, but if the car turns up a few miles away it might confuse them, especially if they find our guns in there." As casually as we could, we strolled away from the car into the gloomy street, taking lefts and rights almost aimlessly until we arrived at the Monument tube station.

Brian fished in his pockets and brought out some cash, feeding the machine to buy a couple of tickets that he said would take us to Liverpool Street and then on to the national rail lines. In the quiet corridors, our footsteps echoed back and forth among the posters which proclaimed how much good the Godhead and his sponsored companies had done since coming to power. Promotion of films had given way to propaganda of firms. When we reached the platform, we joined only four other people who all stood apart from each other and stared across at the opposite platform as if studiously trying to read the good deeds that were displayed over the walls. More so than ever before, it seemed that no one talked to anyone else anymore.

"These stations are under surveillance, like everyplace else," Brian said quietly as we stood waiting for the next tube.

"The RAF will get direct access to them as soon as they realise the car's off the road. If they spot us and get here before the next train, we are, as Shakespeare once said, completely fucked."

I chuckled nervously, trying to glance round surreptitiously in an attempt to spot the cameras. They nestled, black and silent, in the corners of the roof, covered in cobwebs and pigeon shit, but a small red light blinked continuously on all of them and their lenses glimmered in the faint light, awake and alert. None of them seemed to be pointed in our direction, at least none of those I could see, but I didn't feel comfortable until a Circle line train rattled into the station, and slid to a stop. We stepped inside as the doors opened and took a seat.

"Where are we going?" I asked Brian quietly, even though the carriage held only one other person.

"We'll take this one up to Liverpool Street, then we'll get a train out to Romford. All the tube stations have got cameras in them and the RAF'll go through all of them, trying to find where we get out. By going out to Romford, I hope they'll think that we're hiding out there or we've got a contact or something. From there we'll head back into London, hopefully throwing them off our track. Once we get back, I'll take you to someone who can help you sort out your little problem."

"What problem?"

He smiled over at me. "What you're actually going to do with that key,"

Brian and I travelled by tube to Liverpool Street, where we left the underground and headed for the national rail terminal. Throughout the short journey, despite Brian nudging me every time he caught me at it, I couldn't help but look around for cameras, though he assured me most of them were hidden from sight. The state wanted to let the ordinary people know that they were being watched (there were very obvious cameras around all major public areas for "security reasons") but they didn't want anyone to know just *how much* they were being watched. Almost anything could hold a camera lens these days: not just cashpoint machines and ticket dispensers, but little things like light bulbs; the hand rails on steps; the badges in guards' lapels; the handles on the fridges in newsagents. Anything and everything could be used as a surveillance device for the Godhead to keep a watchful eye on his flock, and most of the flock were content to let it happen.

Liverpool Street station was quiet, with only a few people making their way home, mindful of the curfew for those without work or travel permits. In the city centre, the Church Police were a little more lenient, understanding that due to the nature of some people's jobs, there were bound to be some people travelling late into the night. We, however, were not among them, but despite their reputation and unlike the RAF, the Church Police are only human. They get tired; at the end of a long shift, most of them can't be bothered with hassling two blokes on their way home from the pub. The closest call we had walking through the brightly lit station was when one Policeman called over to us.

"Where're you two off to, then?" he said, never moving from the pole he was leaning against.

"Home, officer," Brian said cheerily enough. "Been out for a mate's birthday."

He looked at his watch, scowling at us. "Hurry it up, you've only got forty minutes." Brian waved at him as we walked on, past the closed shops that tried to tempt travellers with ties, socks, underwear and coffee, as if all those things went together somehow.

There was a single guard at the gate for our train who looked at our tickets briefly before passing them back and telling us to get a move on. I felt like a child being sent to bed; the city's officials were desperate to tuck me in so that they could get on with whatever it was they did after I was asleep. I briefly wondered if this was what my father had done.

There was a train waiting at the platform, quiet and still as if it was already sleeping, and for a moment I wondered if it was actually in service. Brian pushed the button to open the door, though, and stepped in as it hissed open like a snake unhappy at being disturbed from its slumber.

The carriage was empty except for an old man wearing

a brown suit that had seen better days, but obviously not for many a long year. He was slumped in the corner of the last seat, his feet up on the cushion opposite him, arms wrapped around his body for warmth or security. His hair was grey and wild, and pale stubble dotted his cheeks and chin giving his face the appearance of having been pebble-dashed. A plastic bottle sat next to him, though whether it contained water, vodka or meths was anyone's guess. At his feet lay an opened, empty tin of cat food, a green plastic fork poking out of the end. He didn't move or look at us as we boarded and took our seats; he just kept staring out of the window at the rail tracks.

Brian glanced at his watch. "Shouldn't be more than a few minutes," he said. He ran his hand over his face, scrunching his eyes up as he yawned enormously. We both slouched in our seats, looking around at nothing and everything, trying to look for all the world like two normal people waiting for their train to pull out of the station.

I sat and waited for it to start, looking out of the window and along the platform every ten seconds or so, convinced that at any second, just before the train started, the white Maltese crosses of the Church Police would be glimpsed as the sharpshooters took up positions; that the voice of an RAF officer would come over the tannoy or a megaphone, telling us that the game was up and that we should surrender; that the windows would shatter as a gas canister burst through, smoking out the carriage as they had the Mason's Arms. I could control that, though; it was when the train was actually ticking over, when we were about to go, when at any second our escape would be certain — that was when I freaked, sitting up in my seat and almost willing the RAF to appear, just to put me out of my suspense.

It took fifteen minutes that felt like a week before the train gave a shudder, its engine grumbling worse than the doors as it stirred into life before it slowly pulled away from the platform.

"Thank Christ for that," I said as we slid out from under the roof of Liverpool Street, into the lamplit night. Brian didn't reply; his head had tilted backwards, his mouth hanging slack as he slept quietly.

I didn't know how long it would take to get to Romford, so I decided to stay awake and watch the stations go past. Five minutes later I was asleep.

*

"Are these touched? Are these touched?"

The old man's voice woke me from the brief slumber I'd fallen into and I stared at his face, which hovered a few inches from mine, separated only by the thin mist which seemed to seep from between his cracked lips, and which filled my nose with the smell of cheap booze.

"What?" I managed, moving my head back. He ignored me and looked out of the window, staring through the grubby, rain-streaked glass. Drops of rain, propelled by the train moving against the wind, ran races with each other to see which one could stay horizontal the longest.

"I'm sorry, I'm not having it. Are these touched? Nothing's touched," he babbled, turning quickly to face Brian who slept on, oblivious to it all. "I'm not having it. I'm not into life swapping. I'm sorry. Are these touched?" I watched as the mad old bugger stumbled against the movement of the carriage and swung from pole to pole, a dirty, dishevelled monkey, asking the same question, repeating the same phrase over and over again to no one in particular. "Are these touched? I'm not having it. Nothing's touched. I'm sorry. I'm not having it."

Brian woke, mumbling a question which, I guessed concerned where we were.

"I don't know. I fell asleep as well," I replied. Brian looked over my shoulder at the old man in the brown suit who was making his way up the aisle, stopping every now and then to look out a window.

"What the hell's he up to?" he asked, rubbing at his eyes, then staring at the man as if trying to make sure he wasn't still asleep and dreaming. I shrugged.

We both sat quietly, Brian staring out into the night, framing his hands against the window and peering through them, shading his vision from the reflections of the carriage interior.

A few minutes later, the train slowed and we came to a halt at Goodmayes.

"At least we haven't missed Romford," he said. The doors hissed open, rain diving in as if it had almost missed the train, but a moment later they closed and the journey continued. The connecting doors between carriages clicked open and I turned to see the old man wandering away into the next section, still repeating his question and answers. "The state of some people," Brian said, settling back into his seat and belching loudly.

*

Romford station, like the others we'd passed through, was silent and deserted and, as far as I could see in the dim lighting, didn't seem to be under the watchful eye of the Church Police cameras. We walked down the steps and into the short subway which led out on to the main road, then turned left into the town centre. As we passed under a bridge, I caught sight of the Job Centre on the other side of the road. It was boarded up, its sign broken and hanging loose from its moorings and the remains of the front door dangling from the hinges. Despite the weeds and graffiti that had grown all over it, somebody had recently put up posters advertising the latest government initiative for young people, encouraging them to enlist in the RAF or the Church Police, offering "financial, emotional and spiritual fulfilment". Someone had succinctly sprayed BOLLOCKS underneath it, summing up the feelings of what could well be the last generation of humans on the planet. With no children being born, the teenagers of today had to unknowingly handle the burden of being the last of their kind and, from what I'd seen of kids over the years, they were going to make a complete balls-up of the job.

Out here, beyond the wall that was still being built around London, the people weren't so easily fooled by the government propaganda. Jobs in suburban and rural areas were almost non-existent as more and more companies, desperate to hang on to the earnings that in a few years' time would mean less to them than they did already, downsized their firms and moved to the capital. They left behind communities of the unemployed that huddled together, hating, envying and fearing those from the city for having taken their jobs away and forcing them to sit and wait for the end of it all.

"The Church Police don't come out this way anymore," Brian said quietly as we walked through the rain, dodging puddles and litter. "The RAF occasionally make their rounds, but even that's becoming rare. They'll do random sweeps, claiming they're looking for drug dealers or arms merchants, all the usual stuff, but really they're looking to get rid of these people."

"Where do they take them?"

"Down south, usually. Or over to the West Country. There are fewer and fewer people left, McKean, who remember the good old days."

"What happens to them?"

Brian shrugged, wiping the rain from his face. As we walked, he kept looking around, though whether he was looking for someone in particular or just being cautious, I wasn't sure.

"I don't know. There's lots of rumours, of course, especially about the camps down south, but I don't think there's many people who actually know for certain, and those that do . . . well, they're the ones in charge and they sure as hell ain't talking about it."

We turned off from the main road and walked down a side street decorated with rusted scaffolding and rotten wooden planks. It leaned precariously against the wall of a building as if for comfort, the pair supporting each other like an old drunken couple caught in the rain after the pub closed. Three or four men hung in the shadows, suspended from the iron network by ropes or electric flex around their necks, their naked bodies twisting slowly in the light breeze. There was no apparent reason for the killings; they didn't wear any placards around their necks; they wore no obvious gang colours; they were just dead men. In the dim glow from the infrequent street lights I could see that all of them had had their legs worried by dogs or cats — chunks of flesh were missing and, from one of them, an entire foot.

"Jesus," I whispered.

"It's not good, is it? The people in London think it's crap there, but hardly any of them come this far out. You should see some of the other places I've been to; fucking South Wales has become a huge factory, churning out guns and stuff for the RAF and the Church. It's just one big industrial complex from Cardiff to the valleys. They didn't bother putting a wall round the city there, just fucking built over it."

"Is that where you're from?" I asked him. He laughed.

"No, mate. I'm from round here, originally, but I ran into a bit of trouble. Wandered around for a bit, you know."

I couldn't help but smile, thinking of the trouble I'd been wrapped up in with the heroin, and the escape route I'd taken. "Yeah, I'm with you there."

"Things got rough round here about five or six years ago," Brian said as we crossed a road, heading for a row of lockup garages. "People found they couldn't claim any benefits when the rules began to get tougher and tougher. Back before the Godhead, all you had to do to get the dole was show you were looking for work. That went out the window soon after he came in, I can tell you. They cracked down on fraud, people who were signing and working, and set them to work building stuff like the RAF holding stations and prisons. More and more benefits were cut: if you were disabled it was your problem for having been born a cripple; if you were looking after someone who was sick, it was their problem for being ill. Me and my brother were on the dole when the Godhead came along. My sister was looking after our mum. She couldn't work and there were no jobs for us, but we still lost what little money the government was giving us when the reforms came in." Brian turned to me, a sad, tired smile on his face.

"No wonder we turned to crime, eh?" He chuckled, looking up at the dull sky that seemed to perpetually rain on us. "Me and my brother started nicking stuff and selling it. We weren't completely noble; I mean, we managed to get our mum's pills and stuff, but most of the money we made we spent on beer and speed. Things carried on like that until we did over this one house, completely cleaned it out, only to find out a couple of days later it was owned by some bloke who was setting himself up as a gangster; you know, bad attitude, getting a 'posse' round him with guns and everything. Arsehole, really."

"Yeah, I know the type," I said, thinking of Roller.

"Anyhow, we robbed this one house and a couple of days later I saw my first Downer. Seems this gangster had gotten himself one of those fucking freaks and found out who'd done over his house. I came home from getting some stuff from the shops and found the burning shell of our house with this Downer in front of it, surveying his handiwork, like. Now the house I could have lived without, I wasn't worried about that. My family, though . . .

"I walked round the corner and just stared at the house along with all the neighbours. Smoke was coming out of the windows, flames were poking out through the roof and the place was obviously fucked. And this Downer stood in front of it, looking up at where he'd nailed my family to the window frames. He'd nailed them up by their wrists, even my mother who hadn't gotten out of bed in the last four years, and just stood watching them burn." Brian fell silent. He opened the large gate that led to a courtyard in front of a set of lockups and took a ring of keys from his pocket.

"What did you do?" I asked as he unlocked one of the garages.

"I discovered you could kill a Downer by taking a handy metal pipe and beating the fucker round the head for a good twenty minutes," he said with a chuckle, and pulled open the door.

*

The car Brian had stored in the lockup took us back to London in comfort, if not exactly in style. Despite the lateness of the hour, we weren't troubled by any of the infrequent Church Police patrols until we neared the city wall which, in the area Brian headed for at least, was still well under construction. The main shell had yet to be erected, so that the scaffolding that stood around what would become the innards of the wall gave the impression less of bare bones and more of the interlocking sinews and fibres of muscles, waiting only for the brick-and-steel reinforced skin that would be draped around their nakedness. As we approached, I voiced my nervousness to Brian, but he merely shrugged and reached into the glove compartment.

"If they have fingerprint or retinal scanners, we're fucked," he said as I took the few forms he handed me; an old-fashioned passport without a photograph; a Church membership card which said I worshipped at the Beacontree Heath Church in Chadwell Heath; and a credit card sized ID, this time with a blurred photo of someone, that told me my name was Pete Campbell. "Hopefully, this late at night, with this car and our natural charm, we should get through any Church Police checks."

"What's so special about the car?"

"It's an RAF undercover vehicle," he grinned, the sparse street lights strobing across his features, turning his teeth a sickly orange. "We picked it up a couple of months back and stashed it in Romford for an occasion just like this. The Church Police should recognise the standard registration, but we better hope they don't check that, either."

I hung my head, rubbing at my tired eyes. As I moved in my seat, my leg throbbed, the barely mended break moaning at me like a spoilt child that hadn't received what he wanted. It felt like almost ten years since I'd last had a decent amount of sleep and a fairly normal life, and what Brian was saying didn't seem to make much sense.

"Isn't that a lot of hopes and wishes?" I asked. He glanced at me. "I mean, we gotta hope they haven't got any scanners, that they recognise the car but don't check it, that the ID we've got will get us through, that it's the Church Police and not the RAF. Jesus, Brian, you're not giving me much confidence here."

"If you want to walk and try to get through like that, it's up to you," Brian said. "Personally, I wouldn't advise it, as there's a checkpoint coming up."

He slowed the car down as we approached, the revolving searchlights from the guard post making the scaffolding glint and shimmer briefly. The shadows moved as the beam swung back and forth before it spotted us, stabbing down in the middle of the road. Four members of the Church Police stepped forward as we slowed to a halt, rifles over their shoulders and not held in front of them. Brian wound down the window of his door.

The young officer looked over the car for a moment, opening a small book she took from her pocket and checking something. "You RAF?" she asked, squatting down to look Brian in the face.

"You better hope we are, girl, otherwise you and your men could be dead by now," Brian said.

"How do you mean?" the officer asked, obviously bored and barely managing to stifle a yawn. She wasn't impressed with Brian's "I'm in charge and you're in for it" speech.

"Rifles on your backs, for God's sake! Kneeling down at my level! We could have taken you all out by now!" Brian's voice misted in the cold air, ghosting over the young woman's face.

"Yeah, you're RAF all right," she said, standing up and waving us on. "Go on, fuck off." Despite what the adverts on the Romford Job Centre had proclaimed, this girl had found none of the rich rewards promised by the Church Police. Instead, she found herself standing around in the middle of the night and waiting for maybe one or two cars to come along.

Brian chuckled, wound the window up and drove through, not forgetting to scowl at the other officers, all of whom ignored us completely. With all of Brian's precautions — the car, the IDs, his bluff — we had made it through a check point purely as a result of the guards' complete lack of interest. If guile and a fake ID wasn't enough, thank God we had the apathy of the Church.

*

The rest of the journey was fortunately short and uneventful. Brian drove for perhaps another hour or so and, though I tried not to, I couldn't help but drift off to sleep. When he woke me by shaking my shoulder and telling me we were here, I had no idea where "here" was.

As best I could, I slid from the car, although my leg yelled at me whenever I tried to put too much weight on it. I followed Brian up the short drive to a detached house surrounded by a neat garden, where only the most recently shed leaves lay on the grass, the rest having been cleared away.

"Don't worry, Aitch," Brian said, as he rang the bell. "You're on the home stretch now." I noticed he hadn't said that *we* were on it, and was about to mention this when the front door opened, the porch light springing to life.

"Aitch McKean, how nice to see you again," the Pale Man said. I stared at him as he and Brian took me by the arms and pulled me inside.

Chapter Twelve

"Fucking hell, now I'm confused," I told the Pale Man.

It was the next day, though I was lost as to the actual date. I knew it wasn't long until Christmas, but there was no way of being more specific until I found a calendar somewhere. With all I'd gone through, I could cope without knowing the date.

Despite my protests the night before, Brian and the Pale Man had led me up the stairs of the house and left me to undress for bed, locking the door behind them as they left. I tried the window as soon as they were gone, but not only was it locked, there were also bars on the outside. I sat on the bed, my leg hurting like hell, and inspected the dressing on my arm. It looked as if it needed to be changed sometime soon, but I figured there was nothing I could do right at that moment and so, my mind won over by the demands of my body, I undressed and got into bed.

It was Brian who woke me up the next morning, shaking my shoulder the same way he had when the car had pulled up outside the house the night before.

"Sorry about locking you in, mate," he said once he saw I was awake. "We figured once you clapped eyes on Straw you'd freak and try to run."

"Straw?" I asked before I remembered Slake telling me his name. "The Pale Man, right."

Brian chuckled. "Hey, all these Uppers are pale, Aitch. You ain't gonna get anywhere if you call them all the Pale Man." He straightened up and headed for the door. "There's some clothes and stuff in the cupboards. Something should fit you. When you're ready, come down to the living room and we'll let you know what's what." Brian left, pulling the door closed but not locking it.

I got up and, as Brian said, found something to fit me in amongst the mass of clothes, both men's and women's, that were folded, hung or just stuffed into the drawers and cupboards that took up one wall of the room. Stepping out on to the landing I saw a door clearly marked BATHROOM, and went in. After using the toilet, I checked myself over in the mirror hanging on one wall.

I looked like a drunken, homeless bum with my stubbled, pale cheeks and red-rimmed eyes sunk deep in their dark sockets. My hair stuck up in whatever direction it damn well pleased and was not going to be coerced or cowed into submission. Both my teeth and my tongue looked as if they could do with not so much a brushing as a scourging. I washed as vigorously as I could, trying desperately to feel clean again. After all that had happened, I wasn't sure I'd ever feel that way.

Dressed and slightly refreshed, I headed downstairs to the living room where Brian and the Pale Man, Straw, waited for me, both of them chatting over cups of tea and slices of toast. The whole scene presented an understated contrast to the home of Slake, the Downer that had "rescued" me from the clutches of the RAF.

"Can I get you a cup?" Straw said, standing up. It took me a moment to get my thoughts in order; I'd never heard him speak before, and his almost Queen's English accent threw me for a second.

"Sure," I said, sitting in one of the two armchairs. Brian sat in the other one while the Upper had the whole sofa to himself. He left after checking whether I wanted tea or coffee and, as we waited for his return, Brian offered me the plate of toast.

"Nothing so English, eh?" he said. "Tea and toast in the morning. Perfect way to start the day."

"I'd settle for a few answers, myself," I said. Straw returned, mug in hand, and sat back on the sofa, handing me the tea.

"What would you like answers to, Aitch?" he asked, smiling despite his best efforts, while Brian, sitting opposite smirked.

"Where to start? Who are you, what do you want with me, why were you working with Roller, why did you kill him and his men and let me and Rhea escape, where the hell is she and most important of all . . . " I took a breath and reached into the pocket of the jeans that had been provided for me, taking out the keyring I'd been carrying round since I'd received it back in America. I selected the nondescript mortise key that everybody had been after without knowing what they wanted, and held it up to him.

"Most important of all," I said again, staring at the Upper, "what's *really* so fucking special about this thing?"

"You weren't told?" He shook his head and chuckled with Brian.

"Guy's carrying the most important thing in the whole world and he doesn't even know what the hell it is," Brian said in disbelief as I looked from one to the other.

"Tell you what, Aitch," Straw said, "why don't you tell us how you got it and what you were told to do with it, then I'll let you in on the mystery. What do you say? I have to admit I'm curious how you came to be holding it. Tell us the story, the true one."

"I've told so many lies about the bloody computer disk and everything that I can barely remember what the truth is."

"The truth, Aitch?" We all turned to look at the speaker. She stood leaning against the door frame, her long black coat wet from the rain that still fell outside though her hair was dry beneath the wide brimmed hat she wore. In one hand she held a cigarette, the smoke curling slowly up to the ceiling, while her other, mutilated hand hug at her side. "The truth would make a nice change, coming from you."

Rhea and I looked at each other; I didn't know whether to be pleased, scared, angry or suspicious, whereas she just stared at me with a hard, dead stare.

"You two know each other, obviously," Straw said, getting up to make Rhea a drink. She shrugged off her coat, revealing her thin frame with the machete still strapped to her leg though now it was on the left hand side. Tossing her coat into a corner and taking off the big knife, she sat on the sofa next to the Upper's seat and stared over at me, only taking her eyes from my face when Straw returned with a mug of tea. He sat next to her, putting his arm around her and giving her a hug.

"The truth, Aitch," Straw prompted.

"Fucking hell, now I'm confused," I told the Pale Man.

*

I recounted briefly the tale I'd told Rhea as I lay in the hospital bed, beginning it in a slow, laboured fashion; I didn't want to be rehashing everything once again. I was tired of the whole damn thing, or so I thought, but as the story went along, I felt my body responding. I became animated as I retold the story of Broken Feather and the Native American reservation, his skill at digging out information from the Internet and the consequent discovery of the figures relating to the lack of births since the Godhead's arrival. But it was when I reached the part about the captured Upper that reality and fiction merged.

"So they didn't kill him?" Rhea asked. I shook my head.

"Not right away, but part of me wishes they had." I looked around at my audience, one at a time. "If it wasn't for him, I wouldn't be here.

"Broken Feather and his friends brought him in to the camp as a prisoner; none of them had seen an Upper in the flesh before. They interrogated him for days, but he didn't have any answers, at least none that satisfied Broken Feather. The Upper called himself Rock, and to say he was confused would be like saying the sun is quite warm. The guy didn't know what the hell was happening, where he was, not only who we were but *what* we were. He didn't have a fucking clue about anything except his mission."

"Which was?" Straw asked.

I held up the key, turning it round, trying to find anything about it which made it stand out from any other. There was nothing.

"Rock claimed to be the keeper of the Key to Heaven, and said that he had to get it to his Father, with a capital 'F'. Three guesses who that turns out to be. Anyhow, Broken Feather held Rock for days after having taken the Key from him, but without listening to Rock's story. I got lumbered with that little tale when I had to guard the sorry bastard." I glanced over at Straw to see if he would give me any validation for the next part.

"See, Rock said that the Upper in this country who calls himself the Godhead isn't just any old Upper, that he isn't the Messiah, that he is in fact, God Almighty Himself, who had somehow been tricked into quitting the throne of Heaven by, who else, the Devil. Because Rock himself had been thrown out at the same time, there was no one left to lock the gates behind him. He'd been wandering round the States for about five years, trying to get someone to take the Key to the Godhead. Trouble was, like I said, he didn't really know who or what we were,"

Rhea and Brian stared at me for a moment, both of them smirking.

"Is that it?" Straw asked.

"Pretty much. Except for this: Rock said that, even though he only held the Key to Heaven, when the Devil stepped into the Godhead's shoes, the door to Hell was left open as well."

"So much for the truth," Rhea said with a sneer. "I thought you didn't believe that story when Hal told it to us?"

"You gotta admit, Aitch, that's pretty far fetched," Brian said.

"What, you walk around with Uppers and Downers and *that's* believable? Christ, I didn't say I believed it, I just said that was what that idiot Rock told me. Either way, when the group was broken up by the ATF, Broken Feather gave me the Key to bring back here and pass on to Jerry along with the disk. It was Jerry who'd arranged for me to meet up with Broken Feather and his bunch; the pair of them knew each other through the Net. While Broken Feather didn't believe Rock's story, Jerry apparently did, and as I was a mate of his, I got selected to take the lot back home."

"Why didn't Jerry just get the information off the Net directly?" Rhea asked. "Why bother with the disk at all?"

"The information was suppressed over here years ago. The net's censored to hell by the Godhead's government. If Jerry had gone looking for it, the RAF would have been on him like a shot. He had to get it on disc from the States, and when Broken Feather told him about the Key, he wanted that as well.

It was Jerry that was supposed to deliver this bloody thing to you, not me, and he would have if he hadn't gotten stabbed by some stupid fuck of a kid!" I said, raising my voice. "I never wanted this thing, and I never wanted to get mixed up in all this cloak-and-dagger crap, either! I don't care what the Key is, what you want it for or what you're going to do with it! You want it, it's yours!" I hurled it against the far wall where it smacked into the paper, sending up a puff of plaster dust.

Brian and Rhea sat quietly after my outburst, while Straw merely stared at me thoughtfully. I slumped in my chair, catching my breath and, once again, found myself wanting a cigarette.

"That's not the most lucid telling of the story," Straw said after a moment, "but it's essentially the truth."

Brian, Rhea and I all looked at him.

"You mean it's true?" Rhea said.

"I don't know about Aitch's side of things, but God being ousted . . . in its basic points, yes, it's true." He sighed when he saw us all staring at him, our expressions like those of dogs being teased by having a ball shown to them but not thrown.

"I think you ought to carry on, Straw," I said.

Taking a deep breath, the Upper began to talk.

"The . . . being, the archetype you know as God, has indeed vacated the heavenly throne and been replaced by what is commonly called, for want of a much better word, the Devil. Don't think in terms of an old man in a flowing robe with a glowing white beard and halo, or some horned beast with a pitchfork and hooves. Those are merely representations humans have conjured up over the years to help them visualise what are two halves of the same coin. There is a force of Goodness throughout the Realms, and, as with all basic dualism, there must be an opposite, a primal force of what you call Evil. These two forces have been personalised and represented in religions across the Realms, but not always in such distinct forms. There have been Gods whose deeds, were you to read of them today, you would consider Evil, yet at the time, by their peoples, they were viewed as being Gods of great Goodness. Call them God and Satan, Jesus and Judas, Yahweh and Baal, Vishnu and Shiva, Atum-Ra and Set, Odin and Loki, they have always represented the same forces, even if not always the ones you would think of.

"But now, God has not only been usurped, but also imprisoned. The Godhead does not run this country. He is an unwilling front man used by the controlling Downers and those who work with them. His legions, those you now term as Uppers, have also betrayed him, eager to join with the Downers in battle upon the earth, to settle once again their war."

"Settle it again?" I asked.

"Indeed. The battle has been fought time and time again over thousands of your years, and not always on this planet." Straw smiled as we let that little titbit filter into our minds. "The Key that you have so hastefully discarded," he said turning to me, "is an icon, a representation. If the Godhead were to regain it, if he could again close the door to what you know as Heaven, then Hell, being not just an opposite, but a reflection, would also be locked, thus stopping the flow of both Uppers and Downers."

"But . . . " Brian began, "how do you get here? You people, I mean?".

"Every time a human being dies, their personality, their being, their soul, if you will, is absorbed into one or the other of the two forces, dependent on how they have lived their lives and their dedication to the truth. In simple terms, they go to Heaven or Hell. When they arrive, as both doors are open, one of the present occupants can be fashioned again into a likeness of that which they once were and returned to the surface."

"So you're saying it's true that when someone dies, one of you guys or a Downer is created, yeah?" I asked. Straw nodded. "So what happens when an Upper or a Downer dies?"

He smiled, almost shyly, like a young girl being asked out for the first time.

"At the risk of endangering my own life," he said slowly, "I can tell you that, when one of my kind or a Downer is killed, a human being regains the ability to either father or bear children."

"How come we lost it in the first place?" Brian asked, a frown on his face. He seemed angry with his boss for the first time since we'd arrived here, and I was willing to bet for the first time ever.

Straw shrugged. "The being you call God is not the only one who works in mysterious ways. The Devil does, also. It could ultimately benefit him, having a situation where no more humans are being born, but they're dying at a steady rate. It won't be long before we Uppers and the Downers are the only ones left. When the last human dies, then the battle will begin again."

"So Broken Feather was right in a sense," I said. "He just thought you were preparing to fight us, not each other."

"The same as Hal," Rhea said, looking at me without murder in her eyes for what seemed like the first time.

"Where does the Church and religion and everything fit in?" Brian asked.

"I think I know," Rhea said before Straw could answer. "If the creation of a Downer is caused by a liar dying, what better way for the Downers to ensure more of them are created than by getting more and more people to lie? If the Downers command everyone to worship at churches dedicated to the Godhead, most of them won't even realise they're lying and so, when they die, after however many years of praying to a God who no longer exists, they'll create Downers."

"Clumsily put, but yes," Straw said. "The people of this and other countries are being told that, since the Godhead has come down to earth, the only way to attain salvation is to worship him as the resurrected Jesus. Religion, however, often bears little resemblance to the truth. By worshipping him as someone he is not, the people are effectively lying, whether they know it or not and so — "

"But how can they lie if they believe they're telling the truth?" I asked. "You can't call someone a liar if they don't know they're lying."

"Semantics do not come into it, I'm afraid, Aitch. The archetype of truth, the presence of Goodness which absorbs your spirit upon death, can be very selective. Why do you think there are more Downers than Uppers? And, with this bastardised religion they have spawned, there will be even more of them in the future."

"So what can we do?" Rhea asked. Straw glanced at her, then turned back to me.

"We need to close the doors to Heaven and Hell. Both of them. If we close those doors, the final battle will be averted for who knows how long and the people of earth can begin to get back to normal. We need to get the Key to the Godhead. As the primary Upper, the first one to appear on the Earth, only he can use it. And that, Mr McKean, is where we'll be calling upon your services again."

I stared at him, then at Rhea and Brian.

"Oh no," I said standing up. "No, no, no. I've been through enough shit over that Key and the sodding disk. I'm through with this. You want to go locking doors, you go right ahead, just leave me out of it."

"What about everything you just heard, Aitch?" Brian asked me.

"Hey, I'm sorry, but all I was asked to do was to bring the Key back here, pass it on to my mate Jerry along with the disk and that was that. He was going to get in touch with someone, presumably you guys, and sort it out. Me, I was just a courier." I turned to Rhea, who glared at me again. "See? What I told Slake was true in one sense."

"You're all heart, McKean," she said.

"Come on, Aitch," Brian said. "You've been through too much not to find out how it ends. You can't just bail out on us."

"Sorry, Bri, but I'm just not interested."

"Of course you are, McKean," Straw said. He stood up, towering over me, and walked to where the key lay. "Jerry was supposed to bring you and your little cargo to the Mason's Arms several weeks ago. Brian would have then brought you to me.

"Haven't you wondered why I was with Roller those times? Why I let you escape from the scrapyard? Why I killed him?"

I stared at him, angry with myself. He was right. He hadn't answered my earlier questions about Roller, and they were answers I wanted.

"So tell me."

Straw laughed. "You're in this, as well you know. But there's another reason I need you. Remember, the Godhead is a prisoner. We have to get the Key to him. He can't come to us. Sadly, though . . . " He knelt down and made to pick up the Key. It moved away from his hand, sliding across the carpet. He tried again, smiling up at me and his actions had the same result.

I looked at him. "What the hell is going on?"

Straw's smile widened as he stood. "The Key likes you, Aitch. You've kept it safe. It doesn't trust me."

Rhea sat forward. "Are you saying that thing's . . . sentient?"

"Not quite. It is an archetype, an icon of something bigger. It's not really alive, but it does possess some sort of ability to . . . link with someone who can protect it. It allowed Broken Feather to take it from Rock and for him to pass it on to you, Aitch, and has let you bring it this far." He grinned ferociously at me, flashing more teeth than a crocodile. "You're the only one who can get it to the Godhead, Aitch. You would have had to come along with Jerry anyway, even if he had made the drop to us."

I stared at him for a second before stepping over and picking up the Key. I tried placing it in his hand, but the thing squirmed in my grip, refusing to touch the Upper.

"You owe me some answers," I told him, the Key clenched in my hand as Rhea and Brian watched. I put the Key back in my pocket as Straw watched me, knowing I was in.

"Fuck," I said quietly and sat back down.

*

At the end of the garden behind Straw's house was a small children's playground. There were only a couple of swings, a roundabout and a slide, but at one point it must have made the child or children of the original owners happy. They must have played in the summer sun without a care in the world, unaware that, before they grew up, the world was going to change out of all recognition. I sat on the cracked plastic seat of one of the swings, my feet firmly planted on the ground; even if I'd lifted them up beneath me and tried to swing up to the sky, the toes of my boots still would have dragged in the dirt. The roundabout, its bright colours peeled and cracked, its body leaning off centre, sat in front of me like an unwanted old man too fond of his cups; he might have been able to tell interesting stories once upon a time, but no one was going to sit on his rusted knees now. Over to one side, the slide still stood, the red plastic faded by the rain and sun instead of by children's backsides, and the steps to the top may as well have been the steps of Heaven: no one was going up them much, either.

I wanted a cigarette, that was about the only thing I was certain of. That and the fact that I didn't want this bloody key that was back in my pocket. Sadly, I wasn't going to get rid of either my addiction or my affliction.

The back door of the house opened and closed and I heard someone walking down the garden path to where I sat trying to think about nothing in particular. On the frosty ground in front of me, Rhea's shadow, tall and straight in the morning sun, joined my own squat, dark little reflection. As if to purposefully contradict my earlier thought, she stepped over to the roundabout and sat down on it, facing me but not looking at me. We sat in quiet, cold silence for a few minutes, and I watched through the clouds sent up by my every breath as she reached into her pocket and slowly, deliberately, almost teasingly, took out a packet of cigarettes and lit one up. With each breath we took, we sent smoke out into the air, and while I wrinkled my nose as the scent of hers reached me, part of me wanted my breath to have that smudged, blue tinge to it, too.

"Do you believe him?" I asked eventually. She hadn't come out just to take in the fresh morning air, I guessed; if she had, she wouldn't have sat next to me, so she must want to talk.

Rhea finally looked over at me. "Why shouldn't I?"

I smiled, thinking back on what Straw had told us. "You seriously have to ask that? All that bollocks about Good and Evil, forces of the universe fighting it out on this and other planets? Keys which decide who they want to be carried by? You believe that?"

"You forget, Aitch, we live in a world where men who look as if they've spent a fortnight in a barbecue oven walk the streets and are accepted. Sure they look different, but hey, there's so many of them, they must be okay, right? Wrong. They're not normal, and neither for that matter are the Uppers, but I know which side I'd rather be on."

I watched as she smoked her cigarette left-handed. She had her right stuffed in her coat pocket.

"The Uppers and Downers aren't normal, you're right. But . . . but this stuff about Good and Evil. I'm sorry, Rhea, I don't buy it. And I'm not sure I go for the 'Downers are bad, Uppers are good line', either."

"Then explain it. Explain the Uppers and Downers."

"I can't!" I said, flinging my arms into the air. "I never said I had all the fucking answers! I just don't believe this black and white, Good and Evil crap."

Rhea looked at me, flicking ash into the wind. I watched as it drifted through the air for a moment before falling softly like polluted snow.

"You obviously weren't brought up in a Christian household," she said, dismissing my statements with a turn of her head.

"No, I wasn't, and maybe that's why I can see that this is all bollocks. And if you're saying you were brought up as a Christian, maybe you'd like to explain that guy outside the city wall? The one you killed and whose car you stole? There's two commandments broken in one sentence."

"Don't try to judge me and my actions, Aitch," Rhea said, her words as cold as the air that they plumed into. "I will make my peace with God when I meet him, and I know he'll understand what I've done and why."

I sat on the swing, staring at her, marvelling at the strength of her convictions and the size of her stupidity. I wanted to laugh, but I couldn't because I was afraid she was serious. "You really believe that, don't you?" I asked her.

She dropped her cigarette on to the ground and smiled as she watched my gaze follow it then, quite deliberately, ground the half-smoked butt into the ground until it was nothing but paper and tobacco tatters. "I believe in God, Aitch. If I didn't, I couldn't have gotten involved with Straw and I wouldn't be willing to go along with the plan, which, by the way, you are a major part of."

I shook my head again, this time in despair. There are plenty of things that really piss me off; fervent believers in one cause or another are way up there on the list. Rhea had originally impressed me as someone who could help me and take care of herself. With religion added to the mix, my respect was waning.

"You just can't seem to get it in your heads, can you? I don't want any part of this bollocks. I've had enough of running around, being chased and shot at. I don't want to take this bloody key to the Godhead. All I want to do is get the hell out of this country again and go back to the States. It's not much better, but at least there are fewer Uppers, Downers and nutters like you."

Rhea stood and stepped over to me. I sat up in the swing, looking at her just as she pushed me backwards, sending me off the seat and thumping on to the hard ground on my back. I swore and tried to get my legs free of the chains of the swing. Rhea stared down at me, her hands in the pockets of her long coat.

"You know what you are, Aitch? You're a whining little shit. You know exactly what you have to do. You know you have to see this through. You've come too far now to ever back out, and you're going to complete this task, this mission, whatever the hell you want to call it. We need you, as much as it galls me to say it, because without you we're going nowhere. So do us all a favour: stop your whining and do what you know you have to do."

Without another word, she walked back to the house, leaving me lying in the frost.

*

"The Godhead will be giving his Christmas address early this year, in four days' time; prior to that he won't be leaving Buckingham Palace except to go to his church. We have to get to him before then. On the day of the address, he'll be surrounded by Uppers, his own personal guards, and we won't have a chance of getting near him. After the address, he's scheduled to be going to Europe to meet with other leaders to talk about the benefits of his rule. We have to get him before then, which leaves us just three days." Straw looked around the table at all of us. "It's going to be tricky if we try to sneak in. We don't know where in the Palace he stays and the security on that place is second to none, so we have to take a more direct route."

"Like what?" Brian asked.

Straw smiled. "We're going to drive a bloody big truck in through the main front door."

"We're what?" Rhea asked, leaning forward. "What the hell's that going to gain us?"

"The undivided attention of the security forces. The RAF will certainly capture us and, after questioning, when we reveal everything to them, they'll bring us before the Chief Minister who, in turn, will take us to the Godhead. From there we're going to have to play it by ear, but that should give Aitch the best shot at getting the Key to the Godhead."

Brian sat back in his chair, his hand over his eyes. Rhea, too, slumped back, a murderous frown wrinkling her brow. I sat as comfortably as I had throughout the whole thing and just smiled ruefully at Straw.

"And that's your plan, is it?" I asked. "That's the carefully thought-out master plan of attack that is going to get me close to the Godhead within three days?"

Straw nodded, sitting back in his own chair. Judging from his expression, he was none too happy about the tone I'd used. "What's wrong with it?"

"One: we don't have a truck." I started counting the points off on my fingers. "Two: we wouldn't get within a hundred yards of the front gate, let alone the front door, before the guards picked us off. Three: even if we did get through and the RAF captured us, there's no way they'd bother with us in time. I spent three days in a holding station before I was even questioned, and that was when they had plenty of time. If they're gearing up for the Godhead's Christmas speech, they're not going to worry about four failed terrorists locked up in their cells. Where was I? Oh yeah, four: even *if* they brought us before the Chief Minister, which I kinda doubt, why the hell would he take us to the Godhead? What are we offering him apart from something which will bring an end to his entire way of life? Oh sure, he's just gonna be in such a hurry to do that. Five: *if*, and that's an even bigger fucking if than the last one, *if* we get in front of the Godhead, what the hell makes you think I'd have even the slightest chance of getting close to him, let alone handing him the Key? Christ Almighty, Straw, you haven't thought about this at all, have you?"

"What do you propose, then?" Straw said, folding his arms and staring at me like a petulant child.

"We get rid of as many of those ifs as possible. You mentioned a church; do you know for certain that the Godhead's going to be in the palace?"

"Not a hundred percent, no," Straw grudgingly admitted.

"So he may be at this church?"

"It's possible."

"Which church? There's fucking hundreds of them in London."

"Spitalfields in Whitechapel. He tends to stay there for long periods, apparently."

"Apparently? Fucking hell, what have you guys been doing while you've been waiting for me to turn up? You should have had all this sorted out by now, not expect me to turn up at the last minute and fucking wipe your arses for you." I pushed my hair back with both my hands and breathed deeply for a moment. "Why do I keep ending up back in fucking Whitechapel? Okay. He could be at this church. Which is more likely, the palace or the church, if we go tomorrow?"

Rhea leaned forward. "We can't go tomorrow. It's too

soon, we're not ready."

"And whose fucking fault is that?" I snapped, pissed off with the whole thing already. "You told me to get my arse in gear and that's what I'm doing." I turned back to Straw. "The palace or the church tomorrow?"

"The church," he said quietly.

"Right, unless anybody's got any better ideas, we go to this church tomorrow and see what's what. I take it you haven't got any plans of the place or anything like that?" I asked Straw. He shook his head. "Figures. You've got all the metaphysical bullshit you'll ever need, but you never once thought about blueprints for a stupid church. In that case, we get there early tomorrow, we have a look round and we take it from there." I stood up and walked out. As I left, I heard Brian's voice.

"Well, he's certainly woken up, hasn't he?"

Chapter Thirteen

Whitechapel. The very name suggests purity and God, a clean place in which to worship at, bowing before the all-loving benevolent deity. Christchurch, too, is clean and simple: a church of Christ. But the building we went to the next day exhibited none of these attributes, and it wasn't only because of the large RAF presence.

The church itself — built hundreds of years ago, its foundations sunk into the remains of the plague pits — loomed over the entire neighbourhood, casting a shadow that was less a reflection of a loving God and more the representation of an angry father readying himself to mete out a just and harsh punishment. The building almost stank of despair, a feeling not alleviated by the dull, grey snow of winter which drifted earthward so slowly that it seemed as if the clouds above couldn't care less whether it made it to the ground or not. The architect, a man named Nicholas Hawksmoor, must have known the effect his building was to have on the surroundings and the people who lived there, he must have; for if he didn't, if the church itself had grown into the twisted, perverted thing that stood over the streets of Whitechapel . . . surely that would be worse? I could understand the idea of a sinister or merely mischievous mason drawing up his blueprints with a wry smile and a chuckle more easily than I could comprehend the idea that a church, once built, could subsequently go bad. Looking at the thing, though, I couldn't make up my mind which of the two scenarios I found more likely.

From the time I'd spent living in Whitechapel with Hal, I knew that, back before the Godhead's arrival, the church had pretty much been derelict; the basement was used as a shelter for the homeless with volunteers dishing out bowls of lukewarm soup to lukewarm souls who were grateful for anything that they received. The cynic within me was surprised at the idea of a church actually performing a charitable deed. With the Godhead's ascension to power, though, Christchurch, like every other holy building in the country, suddenly found itself host to a new congregation of faithful. The first, true believers were quickly joined by those legally bound to attend and, for the first time in years, Christchurch's innards were warmed by more than the heat of cheap gas stoves.

Within a year, however, it was closed to the public and quietly billed as the private residence of the Godhead himself.

People from neighbouring houses were moved, some of them forcefully if you believed the rumours, and the nearby streets were sealed off by huge black gates of the kind previously reserved for the entrance to Downing Street. The RAF, aided and abetted by the Church Police, established a heavy presence around the church and the streets surrounding it, guarding the place around the clock. When we drove past one of the gates, Straw pointing out the nearest guardhouse, I could think of only one thing to say:

"How the fuck are we going to get in there?"

Rhea, sat in the passenger seat, glanced at me in the rear-view mirror briefly before turning to Straw, who was driving.

"He's got a point, Straw. How do we get in?"

He didn't answer immediately, concentrating instead on not crashing the car into the side of an RAF truck that rumbled past. Despite myself, I couldn't help but sink down in the seat slightly, hiding myself as it went on its way.

"Despite Mr McKean's derision of yesterday," Straw said, carefully not looking round at me, "I had taken the precaution of formulating a plan to get us into the place, on the off chance that we would need to. From there, however, we're kind of on our own, and playing it by ear."

"That's so comforting," I said quietly. "What is this plan?"

Straw pulled the car over to the kerb and turned the ignition off. It being a Sunday, there were people walking back and forth, obviously going to one church or another, and what little traffic was abroad seemed to be carrying people smartly dressed in their Sunday best. I had to wonder how the four of us, dressed casually in jeans and jackets — with the exception of Rhea who, as usual, wore her long dark coat and her wide-brimmed hat — were going to get to wherever it was we were going.

"I think I preferred you when you were a whining, pathetic creature who just wanted to go home, McKean," Straw said, turning around to stare at me, and for a moment I saw the face of the Pale Man, the Upper who, according to Rhea, had killed Roller's gang single-handed.

"And I preferred you when you knew what the hell you were doing." I honestly didn't know whether to be pleased or saddened when Straw dropped his gaze, almost bashfully.

"Can we stop the bickering and sort this out?" Brian said. The three of us looked at him. "Well, it doesn't solve anything, does it? We've got to get into Christchurch, and we're sitting in a car three or four streets away squabbling like a bunch of kids."

"You're right, Bri," Rhea said. She turned to Straw. "So, as Aitch asked, what's this plan of yours?"

I saw movement out of the corner of my eye, and turned my head in time to see a curtain twitch in the front room of one of the houses. I remembered my first Sunday back in the country, the day after Jerry was killed, when I'd been wandering around, trying to find a phone box.

"I think we'd better hurry," I said. "People are looking at us." In an almost Pavlovian reaction, the other three instantly looked out of their windows, trying to spot someone peeking at us. "The plan, Straw?" I asked again, trying to get him to concentrate.

He sighed. "There's a deserted pub at the end of this road, you can just see it on the corner." Everyone strained to see the building he pointed at. "The cellar's a converted bomb shelter which was used way back during the Second World War and, as far as I know, there's still a connecting service tunnel between that and another shelter four streets over which opens out right behind Christchurch."

"So we go through this tunnel and just appear outside the church?" I asked, trying hard not to laugh. "Isn't that a little convenient?"

"What do you want, McKean?" Rhea asked, turning round in her seat to face me. "You want to try and take on the

RAF guards by the front door? With what? We've got three handguns and a machete between us. How far do you think that'll get us?"

I shrugged, refusing to be drawn into an argument. Quietly, I said, "All I'm saying is that having a tunnel connecting two air raid shelters, one of which comes out behind the church, is just a little too convenient. It doesn't seem right, that's all."

"McKean," Straw said, his hands on the wheel, "I didn't build the shelters. I didn't build the tunnel. All *I'm* saying is that they exist, and it might be worth our while trying to take advantage of them. If you'd rather me drive you down to Buckingham Palace, I will, but it was your idea to come here."

Brian looked at me. "He's got a point," he said simply.

"Fine, we'll go with it then," I snapped. Annoyed with the whole thing, feeling like I was being set up, I opened the door of the car and got out, followed by the others. The four of us walked down the street, our feet splashing in the puddles that the snowflakes had left by melting as soon as they hit the pavement. We saw a family leave their house, the father and teenage son wearing shirts and ties, the mother in a heavy coat topped off with a dark hat, much like Rhea's, though I doubt she had a machete on her thigh. They stopped and watched us go past and as we drew level, I stared at the son. He was maybe fifteen or sixteen and was, as far as we knew, among the last generation of people on this world. After him and those of a similar age, that was it — no more. The human race was like a candle reaching the end of the wick — surrounded by molten wax, guttering and flickering, ready to be extinguished by the mess it had made for itself.

"Be lucky, kid," I said to him. The mother instantly drew him close as if to protect him from me.

Straw glanced at me and half frowned, half grinned.

When we reached the pub, the four of us paused outside. The place had an old, weathered sign still hanging above the door, proclaiming that it was once called Langtons and that it sold "fine ales and wines", but I was pretty certain the place hadn't poured a pint for many a year. The windows were soaped over and, though the door wasn't boarded up, it did have a padlock and chain securing the handles.

"Now what?" I asked Straw.

"You're not the only one with a key, McKean," he said smugly, pulling one from his pocket. He stepped forward and unlocked the padlock, pulling the chain through the handles and pushing open one of the doors. "After you," he said, gesturing grandly.

I looked into the darkness of the room. With the windows as cloudy as the sky I could see next to nothing in there. I turned back to Straw. "After you," I insisted.

He chuckled and shook his head, stepping past me and into the gloom.

"Lighten up, Aitch," Rhea said, as she too walked in. I waited for Brian to pass me and looked at the three of them standing in what had once been a lively bar, before digging my hands in my pockets and following them.

"What now?" I asked Straw.

"Now you keep perfectly still," he said with a grin. With the hiss of metal and fabric against nylon ropes, about a dozen black-clad RAF troops dropped from the rafters. Red dots appeared on Rhea's, Brian's and presumably on my own head as laser-guided rifles were brought up and aimed at us, and I had no doubt the men were wearing night-sight goggles in which the three of us appeared as green ghosts.

"Down on the ground now!" one of them shouted at Brian, pushing and pulling him.

"Fucking get down! Down!" another screamed almost in my ear. I glanced up at the shadowy figure that was Straw and could almost smell his grin.

"Bastard," I whispered and launched myself at him, dragging him down to the floor and punching and kicking at him before three or four RAF men, all of them screaming at me to get off him and to lie still, pulled me from him, giving me a swift kick in the ribs as soon as I was clear. Straw stood and brushed himself down.

"Could we have some light in here, please?" he asked, and a second later two of the soldiers had large torches shining down at us. "Do you know, McKean, for a moment back there in the car I didn't think you'd believe my tunnel story."

"I didn't, you fucker," I said as genially as I could. "Not for a second, but I couldn't do anything else."

"You bastard! You fucking set us up!" Rhea spat, looking up at the Upper.

"Of course I did, dear," Straw said with a chuckle. "Now then, since you're all so keen to meet the Godhead, why don't we go and see if he's in, eh?"

Chapter Fourteen

The interior of Christchurch Spitalfields stank. New paint, recent varnish and the mist of polish just sprayed hung in the air, the incense of the new religion: the theory being, make everything smell good and it'll convince people it looks like new. The tart smells, though, didn't hide the faint aroma of corruption that still hung around the place. If you looked closely — and as we were marched through the front door and down the aisle I did nothing *but* look around — you could still see where large patches of damp had been covered over with a fresh lick of paint without being treated first. Around the windows — plain clear glass, not stained — condensation had gathered, pale runnels of water leaking over the sill and trickling down on to the floor. Mould grew eagerly along the walls below the windows, a green/blue speckling that seemed to be the closest thing to life in the place. The new floorboards looked good at first glance, but as we stepped over them, I couldn't help but notice that they didn't quite fit snugly together; they were warped, leaving gaps between them which allowed a glimpse into the dark underbelly of the church. Even the altar cloth looked wrong; it was clean, but it was obviously second-hand, the edges frayed and spotted with mould.

At the end of the aisle, above and behind the altar, three huge stained-glass windows looked down on us. I was no Bible scholar, but I recognised the Last Supper at the bottom of the centre panel, and Christ himself at the top. So vibrant and colourful, the windows seemed to be out of place in the forbidding atmosphere.

At every third pew stood a Church Police guardsman in the usual matte black body armour with the white Maltese cross over the left breast. For the first time I wondered if having that white cross didn't actually hinder them: in a firefight, wouldn't the enemy use something as bright as that as a target? Somehow I didn't think any of these men and women would appreciate the question.

Straw led us along the aisle, the six RAF guards from the ambush pacing us, two either side, one in front and and one behind. Before we were taken from the pub, Rhea, Brian and I had our hands pulled behind our backs and cuffed. We'd been led from the old building and piled into the RAF cruiser that I'd seen pass us as we waited in the car, and then were driven a couple of streets over to Hawksmoor's Christchurch. As we were pushed out of the truck I glanced up, and could have sworn that the spire leaned towards us as if God's eye were perched on a tentacle, carefully watching over us. I took a few steps to one side, still watching the spire, which in turn seemed to be leaning towards me and watching me wherever I went.

"Interesting optical effect, isn't it?" Straw said, looking up at the spire himself. "Lord knows how Hawksmoor did it, but the bloody thing always seems to be about to fall on you." With that, he gave me a sharp push between my shoulder blades, propelling me towards the waiting door, the RAF guards with us every step.

When we reached the altar inside, Straw paused and looked up at the stained window. Off to the right was a huge, dark mass of wood which must have started life as some ceremonial carving commemorating a long-ago event. Now the thing had warped, as if succumbing to the church's inbuilt, secret feelings, the wood seeming to have run, varnish and shadows crawling over it, burying its original design, twisting and distorting it into something almost unholy.

Straw turned to look at us. "Well, what can I say?" he asked, spreading his arms, smiling down at us where we stood before the steps. "Brian, it's been a good couple of months. You've really helped out, working at the Mason's Arms and waiting for Aitch to turn up. Shame it all has to end, really." Straw turned then to Rhea and I sneaked a glance at her. She stared up at him, her face as hard-set and as vicious as when she had been strapped to the table in Corben's interrogation room, glaring at me as her fingers were cut off.

"Rhea, my dear, I'm so sorry. I did actually like you," Straw said, "and I'm sorry it had to work out this way, especially after you sacrificed your fingers and everything. I had no idea Corben would do that. If it makes you feel any better,

I really am sorry that everything's happened like this and I'm really grateful for all your help. That at least is true. Most of the rest of it, though . . . " He shrugged and smiled apologetically.

"And Aitch, of course, the man without whom none of us would be here. Things would be a hell of a lot different if you hadn't ended up with that key over in the States, I'll tell you that for nothing. Chances are I never would have met you, and that would have been such a shame."

"You still owe me some answers, Straw," I said. "I still want to know why you were with Roller; why you killed him; how you and Rhea knew each other. I need to know."

The Upper sighed and smiled.

"I was with Roller in case you contacted Hal," he said. "We knew you might get in touch with him and so needed a way of getting close. I played the part of Roller's faithful Upper. After I'd chased you through the car lot, I phoned our lovely Rhea, here," he continued, glancing at her, "and asked her to pick you up and see where you went."

Straw paused and looked around the church as if soaking up the dark atmosphere.

"We knew you had the key, you see. We'd been trying to find Rock for some time, and one of our . . . friends . . . worked in the ATF in the States. He got to question Broken Feather who, despite his reactionary zeal, told them all about you the moment they brought out the first knife. The problem was, we didn't know who you and Jerry were going to contact — us or another group — so we waited until either we could meet you and bring you in, or you got in touch with this other group, in which case we would have had you all arrested. Poor Rhea, of course, knew next to nothing about this. The downside of being a freelancer, eh dear?"

He smiled at me. "Clear?" he asked.

"You bastard," Rhea said quietly. "You two-faced bastard."

"So what about Slake?" I asked. "The Downer who rescued me and Rhea from the RAF?"

"Irony; it's great, isn't it? He runs the genuine group of

revolutionaries. If he hadn't rescued you, we wouldn't have found out about them. If you'd told him what you really had, he would have helped you far more than I. As it is," Straw's smile widened. "he and his friends were . . . purged after the Mason's Arms episode."

I sagged with the realisation of how I'd been fooled, how I'd missed the perfect chance to end this simply because of my suspicion.

"Shit," I said.

A movement behind and to Straw's left made him turn. He stood up straight and the RAF guards snapped to attention. It dawned on me who was walking through the doorway behind the altar and for a second I tensed, determined to try something, to not go down without a fight. At my side I could see Rhea getting herself ready as well. Then the hands of the RAF guards behind us came down hard on our shoulders and all three of us were pushed down to our knees, with the hands quickly replaced by the cold steel of gun barrels pressed into our necks.

A rush of hot air set the altar cloth and the pages of the Bible fluttering as three figures walked through a doorway to the left of a statue of a man in breeches and a cape. They came out of the darkness and into the dim light of the fluorescent bulbs that hung from the ceiling. Straw bowed his head and took a couple of steps to the side, retreating from the fierce heat and presence of the Downer that stepped up to the altar.

He was huge, the biggest Downer I'd ever seen, and the heat that rolled off him in waves made me lean back as far as I could. He wasn't just tall; he was massive. Maybe close on seven feet in height, he seemed even taller from my vantage point, and his body seemed to stretch from one side of my vision to the other, completely blocking out everything else. Beside me I actually heard Brian gulp, swallowing his fear at the sight of this monster who stood above and before us. Each of his hands was bigger than my head, his long, thick fingers flexing and curling almost in anticipation. Behind him, the walls of the church wavered and blurred as the air surrounding him rippled from the heat. The dark suit that he wore moved ever so slightly as he breathed, like the scorched countryside covering the side of a volcano just letting you know there was still life beneath it.

"Jesus Christ," Rhea whispered.

The Downer turned to her and smiled, his teeth white against the blackened mess of his face.

"He doesn't live here anymore," he said. "I'm his land-lord."

Rhea moved back against the blast of heat that rolled out with the Downer's every word, caught between getting her eyebrows singed at the front, and the metal of a rifle at her back.

"I will be glad to answer your questions," he said, his voice steady and measured with no sense of urgency, just infinite patience, "but first I believe one of you has a little something for me?"

One of the two aides that had walked in with him, both of them Uppers wearing plain white robes, stepped forward, a clear plastic box held in one hand. Inside it sat a small cushion: nothing fancy, just a small pillow that could have come from the corner of any sofa. The Upper removed the lid of the box and looked across at Straw.

"The gentleman in the middle. Mr McKean," Straw said. Though the rifle muzzle didn't leave my neck, the handcuffs were unlocked for a moment. "Please put the Key in the box, Aitch," Straw said. I rubbed at my wrists, the timeless first act of anyone who has ever worn cuffs for pleasure or pain and had them removed.

I looked at Rhea whose gaze, blank and ferocious, had returned to Straw. Brian had sat back on his haunches and was looking at the floor. Straw merely smiled at me and nodded at the box that the Upper now held in front of me.

With a sigh, not daring to look up at the huge Downer, I reached into my pocket and withdrew the key. Slowly, I placed it on the cushion in the box. The Upper quickly took it away, replacing the lid and bringing it over to the Downer.

He raised a big, burnt forefinger and pressed it against the box where the lid met the main body. A thin tendril of smoke drifted up, carrying with it the acrid smell of burning plastic as the Downer sealed the lid, the Upper turning it slowly for him. With a satisfied smile, the Downer waved both the Uppers away, looking back at us as his aides removed the box from his presence.

"Now that the formalities are out of the way, we may proceed."

I cleared my throat carefully, aware of the gun at my neck but mostly of the huge Downer in front of me.

"Would you like to say something, Mr McKean?" he asked, his words, deep and thick, rolling out in a gust of heat. I began to sweat.

"I thought the Godhead was an Upper," I said carefully, not really making it into a question. The Downer smiled, his skin cracking slightly, but unlike all the others of his kind I'd seen, there was no leakage from the wounds that opened; they merely fused shut after a second or two.

"He is less a Godhead and more a Figurehead," he said with a throaty chuckle. "We use his features on posters, and in computer-generated images when the need arises for him to appear on screen, as in his forthcoming Christmas address. He is Godhead in name only, I assure you, Mr McKean, and has been for a long time". He turned slightly and grabbed the altar cloth, pulling it off and balling it up, tossing it to one side as it began to smoulder from the heat of his hands, then sat down on the stone dais, his feet still firmly on the ground.

"I am the Godhead in truth," he said, holding his hands out and tilting his head to one side in imitation of the crucified Christ. He chuckled again, placed his hands on the altar and looked at us. "I assume you would like some answers?"

"Who are you?" Rhea asked, her voice firm and direct. I glanced over at her, and before I could stop myself, I wondered why she wasn't afraid; was this all another trick? Was Rhea still in on some sly little game that I knew nothing about? Or could it just be that she was so pissed off at having been betrayed by Straw that she didn't care?

"Oh, everyone would like to know my name," the Downer said with that same game-show host smile. "But there are several things in existence which are very important, Miss Leary: names, keys and doors. Without a key, you cannot unlock a door, but without the name on the door you cannot know which door the key fits. I have never revealed my true name, nor do I intend to start now. You can, if you wish, call me Ishmael."

"The guy from Moby Dick?" Rhea said.

"No, not that unfortunate sailor. Rather his namesake from the Good Book: *Call his name Ishmael . . . his hand will be against every man, and every man's hand against him; and he shall dwell in the presence of all his brethren.* Genesis 16, Verses 11 and 12."

"You don't look the type to read the Bible," I said, instantly regretting my words and the ability I had of saying the wrong thing at the wrong time without thinking about it. The Downer, Ishmael, turned his attention to me once again, his smile still on his face.

"And you, Mr McKean, do not look the type to hold the Key to the Kingdom of Heaven."

"So was all that crap Straw told us about the forces of Good and Evil true, then?" I asked him. He shrugged.

"I've no idea. What 'crap' exactly did you tell them, Straw?" Ishmael asked, looking over at our former compatriot.

"I informed them about the primal essences of right and wrong manifesting themselves upon the material plane and the absorption of the spirit as soon as it transcends the body and becomes ethereal," Straw said, managing to keep a straight face. Ishmael looked back at us and, after a moment's pause, laughed in our faces.

Ever sat on a beach in the middle of summer? Not one of the tepid, seaside resorts of Britain, full of pebbles and candyfloss sticks — I mean a real beach. Just sitting there in the sun, realising you should go into the shade soon before you burn, but knowing you'll just have another few minutes. Staring up into the sun, eyes closed behind your shades, just feeling your body simmering in the hot, fresh breeze that blows in off the sparkling blue sea.

That's what Ishmael's laughter was like, only the hot air that rippled out from him carried with it the stench of burning and, from somewhere deep in my mind, it conjured up the cries of the damned.

"And you believed him?" Ishmael asked us, when his laughter had subsided long enough for him to let some words out, before it bubbled back up and almost left him doubled over, his hands clutching his chest. "Oh, I'm sorry," he said, wiping away a blood-red tear that had leaked from the side of one eye. "but you people, all of you," He chuckled again, then finally regained control of his hellish hilarity and looked at us all again. "I don't know who's the more pathetic: you three for believing Straw, or him for actually believing it himself!"

"So he's lying?" Rhea asked, glaring over at Straw again. This time, at least, he had the decency to turn away from her gaze, embarrassed.

Ishmael shrugged. "I don't know. He believes it, I don't, but does that make either of us liars?" His huge shoulders rose and sank again, and I thought of Atlas moving his back, getting comfortable with the world on his shoulders. "There are no real answers, Miss Leary. Straw thinks we, and I mean all of the Uppers and Downers throughout this big old world, are the embodiment of these forces of quintessential Good and Evil." He glanced over at Straw, a wry smile on his face, then back to us. "Personally, I think it's a load of bollocks."

He looked at each of us in turn.

"Is this the point where you're all expecting me to tell you what everything means? Where I explain to you why I've done everything that I have to get young Mr McKean and his wonderful little package into my presence? Where I reveal the secrets of the Uppers and Downers?" Ishmael laughed. "If so, you're going to be disappointed.

"You see, there is no black and white, Good and Evil situation here. At least, I don't believe there is, though he does." He jerked his thumb over in the direction of Straw who stood, quietly ignoring everything. "We Downers, and the Uppers as well, aren't that different from you people. We come into this world fully formed, granted, but for the first few days we don't know who we are or why we're here. That knowledge comes to most of us fairly quick, thankfully, but as to what we are or where we come from — who knows? I don't. Here in Britain and Europe, and more especially in the southern American states, we're viewed as being either angels or demons, purely because of our appearance and your tenacious grip on the meagre remains of your Christian faith . . . and I'm glad we are, too. Were it not for that, we might have had a far more difficult time integrating ourselves into your societies. We have taken on the roles you people have thrust upon us and just gotten on with it.

"Am I originally from Hell, some place where everyone is being burnt eternally? Damned if I know." He smiled at his own joke. "Is he from Heaven?" Again he indicated Straw. "Don't know. And to be honest, I don't really care. You people have assigned us roles and, to a greater or lesser degree, we have played them. Things are different, though, in other parts of the world. In China and the Orient, the prevailing thought is that we're either dead ancestors come back to haunt the living or some form of mass hallucination. The government over there doesn't officially recognise us, Uppers or Downers. In the Middle East the Uppers are revered, treated as kings for the most part, angels come down from heaven to aid them in conquering the world. Downers don't last long there, though, not long at all. South America treats us much the same, claiming the Uppers are angels, the Downers demons, while in North America there's a mixture of that belief and another that we're actually aliens. There has been so much written on the theory that the Uppers are actually the Grey aliens, the ones that have apparently been abducting redneck arseholes for the last fifty years and shoving probes up their backsides. To be honest, I could believe that of some Uppers I know!" He laughed again, this time directly at Straw, who hung his head and studiously continued to ignore us.

"So which one's true?" I asked. Ishmael sighed.

"I don't know. One, all, none or a mixture. I don't know." He spread his arms wide, very wide. "Here we are in a church. Prove to me God exists." There was an embarrassing silence. "You can't, can you? Not conclusively? Oh sure, you could mention the Bible and Jesus and all that, but the whole of Christianity is based on a book written by men. Again, you could say that those men were writing under the influence of the Holy Spirit, that they were receiving the words directly from God, thus proving He exists. If that's true, why then was the Bible edited and changed? If the people who changed it were working under God as well, that means He changed His mind about a few things. But that can't be true, because God's infallible; if He changes His mind, it means He was wrong the first time which, as I said, can't happen. If the people who altered things did so off their own back, then your religion is a lie; it came from men and not God, thus proving God doesn't exist, because He sure as hell wouldn't let people change His infallible word, would He?"

"But He gave us —" I started, stopping as Ishmael held up his hand.

"Let me finish, I'm on a roll," he said with a devil's smile. "Here we are in a church. Prove to me God *doesn't* exist." Again we waited for him. "You could mention Darwin and evolution and that the world is so much older than Creationists believe, but that's not to say that God didn't start the ball rolling in the first place, that our evolution wasn't guided by His hand, that the Garden of Eden is not meant to be taken literally, but as a metaphor. You can mention science and it's discoveries, DNA and the splitting of the atom; none of that disproves God, it could be used to show that His work is perfect down to the last detail. You can take any and all arguments and proof and use it to prove anything you happen to believe in.

"A wise man once said, and I quote, that *convictions cause convicts; whatever you believe imprisons you*. There are no answers, no one single, unalterable truth that proves you're right. We Uppers and Downers are just like you people. We come into this world full of wonder, find a role imposed upon us by our peers and elders, and strive throughout our lives to live up to people's expectations by doing what they want us to do, by being what they want us to be. I don't know if Straw's hypothesis is right; for him it works, for me it doesn't. Who am I? Call me Ishmael, for want of a better name. Who am I? I'm the sum of all the experiences that I've had in my short time in this world. Who am I? I'm the Devil, according to some people. Who am I?" He smiled. "Maybe I'm just a second rate philosopher who talks too much about things which ultimately turn out to mean nothing because sooner or later, and I hope it's later, I'll be as dead as the dear old dodo. Everything I've thought and said and written will be nothing more than echoes of greater minds. The world will continue on its way, I will be forgotten, and nothing will have changed."

Everyone paused, looking up at the giant "man" who set on an altar to a God he didn't believe in. It was the silence that greets an impassioned confession, after the audience has heard something they weren't expecting. For my part, I admit I was confused; I'd expected some form of devil, a Dark God who was on this earth to wreak as much havoc as possible. I didn't think I'd be confronted by a philosophising agnostic.

"One question," Rhea said quietly. Just about everyone in the room turned to look at her. "The babies, or rather the lack of them. What's going on?"

"Don't know," he said simply. "I know there's a connection between the lack of births of humans and the number of Downers and Uppers, but I don't know why. The only thing I do know is that since the first Upper, the one you all know as the Godhead, first appeared, humans haven't been born." He shook his head. "That's not strictly true, though. Every time one of us gets killed, Upper or Downer, one of you people regains the ability to father or mother a child again. I don't know why, but there's obviously a link. The Godhead's arrival on this world stopped your procreation. Our departure begins it again, and that is where the Key comes into it."

He looked over at me. "The Upper you met in the States gave you the Key, am I right?" I nodded and said that he was. "Did he know what it was?"

"He said it was the Key to the Kingdom of Heaven and that it had to be returned to its rightful owner," I said. Ishmael nodded.

"You see? We come into the world confused, take on ideas that we pick up along the way, and then start living those lives. He probably wandered into a church before you found him, McKean, heard a sermon and decided that was what he was carrying." He grinned. "You have to admit, it's possible."

"So what is the Key?" Rhea asked. I glanced over at Brian who still knelt beside me, his gaze fixed to the floor, a smile on his face. He noticed me watching and his smile quickly disappeared.

"It serves the same function as any other key; it locks and unlocks. If you'd found the Godhead, and I will introduce you soon, who knows what would have happened? I don't, but, at a rough guess, I think it would reverse the situation: Uppers and Downers would stop appearing, children would start being born again, things could possibly return to what you people tried to pass off as normality. I don't know. Of course, I don't want that to happen, which is why I've taken the Key from you."

"Why not just destroy it?" Rhea asked.

"And risk the same thing happening? No, I like my situation, thank you very much. If we destroy the Key, what do you think would happen?" Rhea shrugged. "Exactly. Maybe nothing, maybe something. I don't want to risk that, so I'm just going to lock it away nice and safe where it can do no harm and I can carry on doing what I want to, which is running this little country for a while."

I smiled at him. "So you're just another bad guy taking over? Is that why you killed the archbishop?"

"I had that old man killed because of his views. They ran counter to mine and he still had far too much power, thanks to his position. It had been building up for quite a while now."

"So you just killed him? What about the letters?"

"Letters?" Ishmael frowned at me, his forehead rolling like black stones.

"He had something like D.W.F.M on the cross above his head, didn't he?"

Ishmael and Straw swapped glances, the pair of them

grinning. The Downer turned back to me. "That's the punchline of a joke, McKean. Someone made that up, and the letters were actually D.F.W.M, apparently standing for —"

"Don't fuck with me, yeah, I know," I said, thinking of Jerry telling me the joke in the pub before he died. I'd actually believed him; I'd really thought those letters were put above the archbishop's body. But then, I'd believed so many people throughout this whole thing and that had brought me nothing but trouble.

"Anyhow, McKean, you shouldn't really talk about good guys and bad guys. You know those Downers you saw in that pub, just after you got back into the country? The ones who work for Slake? They're actually the good guys in all of this. They're a small resistance group who want things to go back to normal for some stupid reason. If you'd gone with them, they would have tried to get you to the Godhead a long time ago."

"Yeah, I know that now," I said.

"Enough talking, I think," Ishmael said, jumping off the altar and standing up, flinging his arm out in a dramatic gesture. "Time for you to meet the man the whole of the Western world wants to meet. Time to meet your maker. Time . . . to meet the Godhead!"

Chapter Fifteen

As I'd mentioned, the cellar of Hawksmoor's Christchurch had for many years been used as a shelter and soup kitchen for the homeless of the area, a place where they could come in, get a hot if not particularly filling meal and literally dry out for a while. The stench of old men, many of whom had soiled themselves on a regular basis, hung in the atmosphere, even though the last lowly tramp had been ejected from the place more than ten years before. The walls of the cellar seemed papered with the residual stink of society's casualties and lost children, the smell of men and women, some old, some young runaways. They had sat around Calor Gas fires, spooning thick vegetable soup into themselves, their fingers raw and red from the perpetual cold, huddled together to share the warmth as their clothes dried on them. It was a smell of mould, of mustiness, of too many damp people in a crowded room like worshippers on a Sunday, huddling in the pews after walking through a downpour.

Ishmael led the way, followed by Straw and two RAF guards, then Rhea, me and Brian, our hands now free of the cuffs, each of us with an RAF man or woman watching closely as we followed the huge Downer. He had to perpetually stoop to get his bulk through the corridor, and even Straw once or twice brushed his head against the ceiling.

The corridor, deserted except for us, didn't only smell of damp bodies; the walls ran freely with water, glistening in the light of the electric bulbs hanging from the ceiling every couple of yards or so. They gave the impression that we were walking through the interior of a body, sidling our way along a piece of the major intestine, the smell of decomposing and digesting food leading us on to the guts of the place. I had to put my hand over my nose at one point as we passed a vent which belched forth a hideous stench of vomit and faeces, and I couldn't help but imagine some dead wino lying below the vent in an underground chamber, his last meal drying and caking on his chest as his legs twitched, vainly trying to free themselves from the sticky mess in his trousers.

"What the hell is that stink?" Rhea asked, pre-empting my own question. Ishmael didn't answer, but Straw turned slightly to reply over his shoulder.

"There's a lot of work going on in these chambers at the moment. Some of it involves re-routing old sewerage pipes."

"What's the work being done for?" Rhea asked. I noticed she held her own hand over her nose and the sight of her stunted fingers made me wince with a mixture of regret and guilt.

"We intend to hold a few more people down here where we can keep a close eye on them, apart from the Godhead," he said with a grin. "There's an old saying about keeping your friends close and your enemies closer."

"There's also one about keeping your mouth shut," Ishmael growled. Straw dropped his gaze to the floor and followed meekly.

Soon Ishmael and Straw were once again able to straighten up as we entered a central hall beneath the church. It was circular and wide, maybe thirty or forty feet across, with four doors in the walls, each one at a point of the compass. Off to one side were four men in overalls and hard hats digging away at a section of brick and concrete and, to my surprise, there was an Upper standing over them, dressed similarly but obviously in a supervisory role, complete with clipboard. My surprise came from the fact that this Upper was very obviously female.

In all the years of observing Uppers and Downers walking around on the face of the planet I'd never heard of, let alone seen, a female of either 'kind'; every Upper or Downer I'd encountered or seen had invariably been male. But here, standing in front of us, as tall and as pale as Straw, was, essentially, a woman. She looked up from her clipboard at our approach, and I saw that her skin was flawless like that of every other Upper and her hair hung in a white bob. She was slimmer than Straw but, like those of a normal woman, her overalls swelled at the breasts and hips.

"What can I do for you, sir?" she asked Ishmael, glancing around him at us, ignoring my open-mouthed look of shock.

"I'd like a quiet word with our guest, if I may. Would you mind taking your crew back out to the main entrance?" She nodded once and, while we waited, helped her workers gather together anything that couldn't be left behind for one reason or another, then walked out into the corridor, ducking her head as she went through the doorway.

"I've never seen a female Upper before," I said, watching her go. Ishmael nodded at the RAF guards who had walked down with us and they followed the workmen into the corridor, leaving Rhea, Brian and me with Ishmael and Straw. They knew we weren't going anywhere.

"That much is obvious, Mr McKean," Ishmael said with a smile. "The look on your face belies your need to inform us of this."

"Where's she from?" Rhea asked. "I have to agree with Aitch: I've never seen one before, either."

Ishmael walked over to where the men had been working and picked up a large brick, brushing the loose dust and cement off its surface. "It's a sad fact that there are so few females of our kind, of either kind, that come into being. If there were more, perhaps this ludicrous link of your deaths and our births could somehow be avoided; maybe we'd be able to reproduce in some way and there'd be no need for all of this."

"Reproduction without genitals has gotta be tricky," I said with a smile at Straw, thinking of Rock, the Upper in the States.

Ishmael shrugged, turning the brick around in his hands, continuing to clean it off, strolling back over to us. "And wouldn't it be better if none of this unpleasantness were necessary?" he said, ignoring my comment. "If our two peoples could just learn to live together?" Ishmael smiled at us. "Of course, that can never happen as long as we have self-styled counter-revolutionaries within my government intent on upsetting the status quo just because they don't like the fact that I have control of this place and they don't. Isn't that right, Straw?"

"Sorry?" Straw said, looking completely confused.

Ishmael grinned. "It's okay. Double bluffing." With an almost casual swing of his arm, he pitched the brick through the air, sending it smacking into Brian's head. There was a loud *crack!* as the stone block connected with the side of Brian's skull. A thin arc of blood shot up briefly as a hole opened up in his flesh, before he crumpled with hardly a sound, the brick joining him on the floor. Rhea and I both knelt at the side of him, she cradling his head and looking at the damage, leaving me to look on helplessly.

The heat building around us warned us of Ishmael's approach but, though I got out of the way, Rhea stayed where she was, glaring up at the approaching Downer. "What the hell did you do that for?" she demanded.

He grinned and reached down for Brian, then began rifling through his clothes. After patting down one arm, then the other, he roughly turned him on to his stomach, ignoring Rhea's indignant cries, laughing as he found what he was looking for. He pulled a large knife out of a sheath that Brian had attached to his belt, its blade glinting in the light. "I knew he'd been too quiet throughout all of this," Ishmael said, pocketing the knife himself. "He just had that look of someone planning something, staying quiet and out of the way, hoping I'd not give him a second thought."

He stood, looking down at Brian's comatose body. "I think he figured if he can't get the Key to the Godhead, then he'd just as soon kill him and see what happens." He tutted and shook his head sadly, then reached down and snatched Brian up from where he lay, pushing Rhea to one side to do it. I grabbed her and restrained her as Ishmael lifted Brian up by his head, one of his huge, blackened hands encircling the man's battered skull.

The smell wafting from the corridors of old men, soup and clothes was usurped by another almost instantly: the smell of roasting meat and burnt hair. Smoke curled from between Ishmael's fingers, followed by tiny licks of flame that spurted up to the ceiling as if trying to reclaim the vapours that rose from beneath his hand as Brian's head began to cook. Rhea turned away, but I watched, transfixed by the sight, unable to take my gaze away, even when Brian's eyes bubbled in their sockets, one popping and dribbling down his cheek, the other actually being launched from his skull, trailing the nerve behind it, diving down into the dirt. His tongue flopped out of his mouth as steam poured out from between his lips, followed by a groan that fluttered up from his throat on the hot air, making me hope that that was all it was: air rushing through his vocal chords. I hoped to God that Brian wasn't somehow feeling this even though he was unconscious. His legs twitched a couple of times and urine squirted down his trousers, his final offering to the world. A moment later he was still.

Ishmael had to struggle to get Brian's head unstuck from his fingers and finally resorted to peeling parts of his skull away with his other hand before Brian fell once more to the floor.

"Now then," the Downer said, "shall we continue?"

"Why Brian?" Rhea asked, a single tear running down her face. "Why not me?" She pushed her coat back and revealed her machete. "Why not take this off me?"

Ishmael smiled, secure in his arrogance.

"Because you, my dear, though ever resourceful with your wonderful coat of tricks, have a brain inside your head — as opposed to all over my hand — which you actually use. You know you don't stand a chance if you attack me directly. You know that Mr McKean was due to use his Key in some way. You know that only that can end this state of affairs, that merely killing the Godhead won't work. You know that in your heart. So you're not going to kill him, are you?"

Rhea stared at him for a second before she shook her head sadly. "No, you bastard. I'm not."

"And you, Mr McKean," Ishmael said turning to me, still picking bits of Brian's head off his fingers. "You are, as you have so vehemently stated through all of this, nothing more than a courier. Is that right?"

I nodded, looking down at the floor.

"I'm glad we have that settled, then. Now then, shall we see the man, sorry, the God, that we've all come to see?" Ishmael led the way over to one of the doors and pulled it open, exposing a short corridor than ran between the wet walls until it ended in another door. A light shone from the room beyond, through the bars that were set in a square at the top — the gentle, flickering glow of a candle. I turned to face Ishmael who stood patiently holding the door.

"Please, go on," he said.

"Aren't you coming with us?" I asked.

He shook his head sadly. "No, unfortunately not. You see, the Godhead and I have a mutual dislike which prevents us from coming . . . face to face, shall we say. But please, you pair go along. I trust you," he said with a grin. He knew full well there was nothing we could do. "You will, of course, need this," he said, reaching into his pocket and pulling out a credit card-sized piece of plastic that smoked between his fingers as he held it. "It's for the lock on the other door. Make sure the black strip is facing right, and run it down the side." Like an impatient father hurrying his children, Ishmael ushered us into the corridor, closing the door behind us.

The glow through the bars was the only light source and we headed for it slowly, our hands touching the walls on either side, feeling the damp solidity as we inched forward.

"What the hell are we doing, Aitch?" Rhea asked, uncertainty tainting her words for the first time. Throughout everything she had been the strong one, sure of where she was going, what she was doing and why. "We could be walking into a trap, here," she said.

"I don't think so," I said quietly, the plastic key card held tightly in one hand. "There's something up ahead . . . something about . . . "

We were perhaps five feet from the door when an almost physical sense of well-being, a feeling of peace and contentment, a wave of basic goodness washed over us. I couldn't help smiling; there was no way I could stop myself. I turned to Rhea, a huge grin on my face, only to find her looking back at me, smiling herself. We took the last couple of steps up to the door and, as I ran the card through the security lock, I felt tears of joy running down my cheeks. Everything would be okay, I had no doubt of it, there seemed no way that anything could go wrong either now or in the future: the entire world was going to work itself out.

Neither of us looked through the bars in the door before we entered the room.

Chapter Sixteen

I knuckled away the tears in my eyes, trying to focus. The candlelight glowed and refracted through my tears, turning the entire room into a sunlit jewel, the walls and meagre facilities blurring into a haze of golden facets. Slowly, as my eyesight cleared, the feeling of euphoria dropped a little; I still felt good, but I wasn't convinced that all the wrongs in the world would be righted. "Bloody hell," whispered Rhea, wiping rather moist eyes as well.

"It can get to you, can't it?"

We turned to face the speaker as, behind us, the door eased closed.

An Upper sat on the small bunk that rested against one wall. His legs were crossed, his feet tucked under his thighs and he held a book loosely in his hands as if we had interrupted his reading. He wore only a pair of light blue pyjamas, the arms and legs of which were obviously too short for him; his wrists poked out ludicrously, as did his ankles. His white hair hung in a long flowing mane over his shoulders and chest as well as down his back, and he smiled at us with what I could only think of as infinite patience.

"Jesus," Rhea whispered.

"No, I'm afraid not," the Godhead said.

We stood and stared at him, wondering what to do. We had come all this way, gone through everything, all the fights and murders and corruption and betrayal, to end up in a small cell with an Upper who looked as if he were happy to spend the rest of his life sitting there, reading his book.

And it obviously wasn't the first. An entire wall of the cell was lined with paperbacks, stacked flat one atop another. Many of them were bloated and warped due to the damp, their pages fat and heavy with mildew and water, bursting from the confines of their covers as if the words they contained were too important to be restrained. There were seven, eight, nine columns of books, each one holding maybe sixty books of different sizes; I did the quick calculation in my head, then doubled it as, looking closer, I found the entire collection had been placed in front of another set. Over a thousand books sat against the wall, quietly rotting, their words having been digested by this lonely figure, who had then left them to decompose in silence. A thousand books. I didn't know whether to be amazed by the number or disgusted by the waste.

"It *is* a shame, isn't it?" the Godhead said, following my gaze to where the books lay. "I did ask for a bookcase, but I was told I couldn't have one."

Rhea and I stared at each other, still unsure of what to do or say. After a few moments — and I like to think it was to force us into speaking and not because he was just plain ignorant — the Godhead looked down and continued reading.

"What was that?" I asked him. He looked up. "Out there, in the corridor?"

He smiled. "Yes, it's a bit disconcerting for everyone, really. It's apparently a . . . feeling I give off, something that resonates from me, a feeling of happiness and contentment. For some reason it's concentrated itself in the corridor, I think, perhaps, as a way of preventing Cain from reaching me."

"Cain?" Rhea asked.

"The large Downer. About seven feet tall, very wide. Burly chap. You must have seen him."

"He told us his name was Ishmael."

"No," I said. "He told us to call him Ishmael. He wouldn't give us his real name."

"And a wise thing that was too," the Godhead said, returning to his book.

"You're obviously not going to give us your real name," I said, making him look back up at us. "So what do we call you? Godhead?"

He smiled, the expression a little too condescending for my liking. "That would be best, I think. Quite apt."

Again a silence slipped in between us, like someone gently easing their way in front of another person in a queue who's too polite to mention it. Rhea and I glanced at each other again, the pair of us baffled at his behaviour. This was a conversation which was going nowhere.

"So . . . do you just sit here and read?" Rhea asked him.

This time he didn't even look up from his book, which he'd returned to, just murmured that that was indeed all he did. "Don't you want to escape?"

"Not particularly." He turned a page.

"Why not?"

The Godhead sighed dramatically and stared at her. "Because if I escaped and went into hiding, how would you find me?" We stared at him. "You're obviously not very bright, either of you, are you? If I wasn't here," he said slowly, as if to a pair of children, "how could you find me and bring me the Key?"

For the first time since I'd walked into this small, damp cell full of rotting books, I grinned with a feeling from within. The euphoria was gone; my cynicism was rising as I looked at this all too-frail God.

"So you're waiting for the Key?" I asked him.

"But of course. The fact that you're here obviously means that somehow you must have defeated Cain, sorry, Ishmael, and have come to call an end to this whole state of affairs by bringing the Key," He looked at us patiently. "I'm just waiting for one of you to produce it."

Rhea sneered at him, disliking his attitude as much as I did. "We don't have the Key. Ishmael has it," she said.

I could have laughed out loud at his expression of bored indifference crumbed beneath the weight of her words. The Godhead's bottom lip actually quivered as he stared at her, realisation dawning on his bright face that we weren't here to rescue him or to do whatever he thought we were here to do. The book he had been reading slipped from his grasp and plopped on to the damp floor, landing face down. I glanced at it and read the title: *The Lady Ate Sweets The Day She Died*. For all his cultured voice and arrogance, the Godhead was reading a pulp crime novel.

"You don't have it?" he asked, a single bright tear sliding from the corner of one eye and gliding down his smooth cheek. He looked around the confines of his cell, then bent his head and held it in his hands as he quietly wept.

"Come on, Aitch," Rhea said, making for the door. I

stopped her.

"What would you have done with it?" I asked him. The wet sound of snuffling was my only reply, so I walked over and, taking hold of his hair, pulled his head up. He looked at me as his hands fell away, his eyes now running with tears, the pale golden drops flowing down his face. Even his snot was tinged with gold as it hung from his nose. "The Key. What would you have done with it?" I asked him again.

"Locked . . . locked the door," he said in a voice thick with self-pity.

"That door?" I asked him, pointing back at the one Rhea and I had come through. He shook his head, wincing as the hair I held was pulled.

"No . . . the one inside me." He brought a hand up and feebly knocked against my arm. I let his hair go, watching him as he wiped at his nose like a kid who'd had his arse smacked. "I need the Key . . . to stop all this."

"All the Uppers and Downers?" He nodded. "Why you? What's so special about you?"

He looked up at us, his eyes red and sore, his cheeks streaked with the snail trails of tears, a small fresh rope of snot hanging from the end of his nose.

"I think I'm God," he said.

We waited, Rhea and I, as the Upper, the Godhead — hell, maybe even God himself — wiped at his nose again and tried to compose himself.

"That's why I haven't bothered escaping. I knew someone would get the Key to me. The Gatekeeper would find someone to bring it to me even if he couldn't and it would take years. It's linked to me, you see?" He looked up at us, this second-hand, second-rate wannabe God, almost begging for our understanding.

"Pretend we're stupid and we don't know anything," I said harshly. "Tell us."

The Godhead snorted and hawked a moment before spitting out a gob of phlegm. It landed in a small pool at the end of the bed, slapping wetly against the floor. He shrugged.

"Maybe I am what you'd call God. Maybe I'm not. I

don't know. I think I am. I arrived here ten years ago and was instantly treated like your Messiah reincarnated. I was the first Upper to appear and everyone wanted a piece of me: prime ministers, presidents, popes. Before I knew what was happening, I was at the head of a new movement and up for election for the job of prime minister. Sure enough, I won. I don't know how — religion and politics have never really mixed — but there I was, in charge of Britain. I tried my best, but my heart wasn't in it. I had no interest in ruling this or any other country. To be honest, I just wanted to go home." He looked at us with his sad, puppy-dog eyes. "Trouble was, I didn't know where home was.

"So I was in charge, at least in name. The other people in my new party, they took care of everything, making sure that nothing went wrong, at least for them. Ha! They were nothing but typical, selfish humans; they jumped on my bandwagon, as I believe the expression goes, took as much as they could possibly get, then ran, leaving me with a country worse off than when I'd been elected.

"That was when Cain arrived.

"You people, you always think that Uppers and Downers are two side of the same coin, that we're some kind of brothers. Cain was the first of his kind I'd ever seen. I'd never heard of them before, didn't know where they came from any more than I knew where I was from. But he appeared and, because we were both different from you people, I took to him; I liked him. He offered to help me get things back on the straight and narrow. All I had to do was appear as the kind and loving reborn God the people wanted me to be; the hard work, the governing, dealing with politicians and everything, he would do that.

"He dealt with them, all right. Within six months of his coming on board, Britain was a single-party state. Every other politician had either joined ours, resigned from public office or, in more than a few cases, disappeared or been found dead. It was as easy as that for him. Before I knew it, Cain was in charge and I was just a figurehead. As soon as he could replace me with stand-ins and false computer images, I ended up down here.

"Cain instituted the RAF and the Church Police. He approved the regulating of church attendance and a single religion for the state, not so much on religious grounds but because it was a way of controlling the people. He doesn't like loose cannons. There are apparently places down in the south where people who have refused to worship what he calls the one true religion are sent for re-education." The Godhead looked at us. "They are nothing more than Christian concentration camps. People are killed there daily by the thousands in an attempt to speed up the re-population of this world by others such as himself or me. He doesn't care about the religious side of things; all he wants is power, and subjects to lord over."

"The Key. Where does it come into all this?" I asked.

"It's the Key to Heaven. In all my years in this hole — and I mean the world as a hole, not just this cell — I've known, deep in my soul, that the Key is out there, somewhere, and that it would make its way back to me. I had complete faith that sooner or later, someone would bring it to me and end this madness. I don't know why; I don't have all the answers. I didn't want to hurt anybody. I just got carried away with the flow of things. I just want to end everything. I'm a tired, frightened person who just wants to go home. I don't know why I'm so special. I just want to go home, that's all."

The Godhead put his head back in his hands and began sobbing again, his whole body shaking as he plumbed the depths of his despair.

"That's the problem with good guys," I said to Rhea. "They're all so fucking weak."

I stepped forward and kicked the Upper's leg to get his attention. When he was looking at me, I reached into the inside pocket of my denim jacket and took out the Key to Heaven.

Rhea and the Godhead stared at it.

"But — ?" Rhea said, cutting herself off in mid-sentence.

"Remember the key Straw used to unlock the pub door, where we were ambushed?" Rhea nodded. "When I jumped him, I grabbed it; I used to be a damn good pickpocket when I was a kid," I continued, remembering Qizilbash's lessons. "That was the key I gave Ishmael, the key that he's sealed up in a box never to be used. This," I said, waving it gently as I held it between my finger and thumb, "this is the real McCoy."

"You tricked me!" the Godhead hissed.

"Serves you right for being such a stuck-up bastard in the first place, and for being such a big fucking pussy in the second," I said with a grin. "Now, Mr I'm-So-Innocent: where'd you want it?"

He glared at me for a moment, but it didn't work and he knew it. We'd seen him blubbing like a child; he wasn't impressive, he was just weak. He sat up straight, his feet touching the surface of the cell for the first time, and opened the jacket of his pyjamas.

"Stick it in my chest," he said. "Turn it clockwise once."

"But you'll die," Rhea said.

He shook his head. "The King never dies, my dear. I will return to wherever it was that I came from in the first place, and then you can have this stinking planet back to yourselves," he said. "Breed your mewling little cabbages, pollute the air, poison the seas, purge the land, do what the hell you want with it. I just wish I'd never come here."

"Yeah, me too," I said, plunging the Key into the centre of his bared, scrawny chest. It pierced his skin easily, light shining out from the edges for a moment until I turned it clockwise, all the way round.

The light shut off. The Godhead gave a last sigh and fell backwards, dead, the Key still sticking out of his chest for a moment until, with a small sound like a teardrop of ice falling from a snowman's eye, it gracefully fell apart, crumbling over his skin.

"What now?" Rhea asked after a moment.

A roar of denial and rage rang out along the corridor, rattling against the closed door. Ishmael somehow knew what had happened, that I felt sure of.

"What now?" I asked her back. "I have no fucking idea."

Chapter Seventeen

The Devil roared out his anger as he charged up the corridor and slammed into the locked door of the cell. He pushed his face up to the bars and stared in at the pair of us and the corpse of the Godhead.

"What have you done?" he hissed. Tiny licks of flame spurted from the edges of his eyes and sparks flew from his teeth as he spoke. "What have you done?"

Rhea and I stood in the room and looked back at him, neither of us knowing what the hell to do in the face of such fury. Ishmael moved back from the door slightly and pushed at it with both hands, one either side of the barred opening. Even in the dim corridor we could see his face, his rage lighting up the blackened and blistered skin, tongues of flame dancing around his head as he pushed with all his might against the wood of the old door.

I looked at Rhea. "Your machete. Get it ready." She pulled the side of her coat back and lifted the blade from its magnetic scabbard, standing to one side of the cell door. If I could, I'd make Ishmael regret his arrogance.

I glanced back at the door and saw two smoking patches appearing on the inside where Ishmael's hands were burning through. Frantically looking round, I grabbed two of the sodden paperbacks that the Godhead had left to rot against the wall and stood, one in each hand.

With a cry from Ishmael and a sharp crack, the door gave way, but only where his hands had burnt through; the remainder of the door stood as sturdily as ever. The Downer fell forward, crashing into his side of the door, his hands and arms poking through, hopelessly trying to reach us.

I jumped forward and grabbed one of his arms, using the two damp books as insulation from the tremendous heat. Leaning back, away from his other hand, using my body weight to prevent him pulling his arm back through the hole, I looked over at Rhea.

"Now! Do it now!" I yelled.

"What are you doing?" Ishmael screamed at me.

Gripping the hilt of the blade in both hands, her good left one wrapped around her maimed right, Rhea brought the machete down, severing Ishmael's arm at the elbow just as I let go, rolling away towards the bed.

Like that of the Downer at Jerry's house, his forearm shot across the room, propelled by the explosion of searing hot matter that passed for blood in a Downer. Hot droplets rained down and spattered all around us, hissing as they died in the pools on the floor. Others landed on us and we quickly brushed them off, burning ourselves in the process. Ishmael's arm went the length of the cell and plunged into the columns of books, where it stuck out and turned the dampness within the leaves to steam almost instantly. A huge gout of lava blood poured into the room from his stump before Ishmael fell backwards, dragging both his arms from the door. The cry of a falling angel was ripped from his throat as he rattled his way back down the corridor, crashing into the walls. Steam and smoke filled the cell as the books nearest his severed arm dried and began to burn in a matter of seconds, so huge was the heat from the lost limb.

Rhea picked me up and pushed me over to the door. "Unlock it," she coughed. I scrabbled for the key card and managed to get the thing in the slot. I pulled it open and we lurched out into the smoky corridor.

Huge splashes of Ishmael's blood still decorated the walls and floor, glowing red in the gloom, allowing us to see where we were going and enabling us to avoid them. From the chamber beyond came great choking cries and, as we stepped out into the circular chamber, we came upon Straw and Ishmael.

Straw sat cross-legged in a heap, a huge charred hole in his gut where Ishmael had collided into him with the remainder of his arm, his innards burning away before the onslaught of the Downer's searing blood. He looked down at the smoking hole, beams of light pouring out from the edges, then glanced up at us and quietly asked "Why?" The light slowly faded as he stared up at the ceiling, a look of pure surprise on his face as if, even in death, he could not believe what had happened.

Ishmael knelt on the floor, cradling the wound which

even now bled continuously, great folds of molten flesh rolling over the fingers of his ineffectual hand to pool on the floor beside him. He turned to us as we entered carefully, the flames around his eyes gone, leaving only smouldering, dark pits.

"You bastards . . . you've killed me . . . you've killed him . . . you bastards," he gasped. He tried to stand up but fell back to the floor, his knees cracking sharply against the stone. "Do you know . . . what you've done?"

"We've won," I said grinning as I watched his life's blood drain from his arm.

"You've won nothing," he hissed. "There's others like me . . . just wait . . . wait and see." He gasped in pain and tried to stand again, not even making it off his knees this time. "You bastards . . . I could have . . . could've made this country . . . great again." He groaned and keeled over, rolling on to his back, finally letting go of the stump of his arm. "I could have . . . "

We never got to find out what else he could have done as, with a last sigh, his huge frame simply stopped moving, a final trickle of molten blood bubbling from his arm before that too came to a halt with a small hiss.

"Shit," Rhea said quietly, looking down at the corpse of the huge Downer.

"We've got to get out of here," I said, with a glance over at the door through which we'd all originally entered. "There's going to be RAF troops coming through there any minute. They must have heard him yelling."

Rhea looked over at the hole the female Upper and her team had been working at and trotted over to it. "There's a pipe down here. It stinks like hell but it should come out somewhere."

I walked over, not liking either the smell, the idea of walking through whatever was causing it, or our limited options. But I nodded.

"It's the only way out except through the RAF. I guess we've got no choice," I said. Bending down, Rhea climbed into the hole. I followed her, casting a last glance back at the carnage we were leaving.

"Fuck. I think we just killed God and the Devil in under five minutes," I whispered, before dropping down into the filth below.

*

Ever made a big mistake? Ever just gone along with a spur-of-the-moment idea and regretted it instantly? Ever leapt before looking and realised that there's actually some sense in that old adage? Yeah, me too.

I slipped and slid down an incline until I landed with a splash in a running stream of sewerage. God knows what was in there, but I felt lumps brushing against my legs in the freezing water, sticky masses wrapping themselves around my thighs as I stood and looked around for Rhea, trying to find her in the darkness. I stood in the small pool of light that shone through the entrance hole, but everything else around me was invisible, submerged into the black and Rhea was somewhere in it.

"For fuck's sake get out of the light!" she hissed almost in my ear, her hand reaching out from the darkness and pulling me further down the sewer pipe. Instantly I was sightless. I could almost feel my pupils expanding to their widest point in order to let in as much light as possible, but we were as blind as bats without echo location.

"Where are we going?" I asked her as she pulled me along the pipe, far too fast to my mind. I sure as hell couldn't see anything, so I doubted if Rhea could. She didn't answer, just kept a hold of my jacket as we splashed through the filth, trying not to think of where, originally, it had come from.

Suddenly small beams of light appeared around us, dancing and weaving like drunken fireflies, and as we staggered and ran, I glanced back. Coming through the hole that we had used looked to be three or four RAF troops, their helmet and shoulder torches swinging and bobbing as they went down the slope of the pipe before straightening out and coming after us.

"Rhea," I said, about to tell her we had company, when I noticed four small red dots bouncing around the walls as well, briefly touching us before wandering away again. There was a loud CRACK! and almost at the same time someone punched my right shoulder, or at least that's what it felt like. I spun forward and down, watching amazed as a thick spurt of blood, my blood, shot out from my arm before I ended up in the water and shit in the bottom of the pipe. I landed on my back and went under, instinctively closing my mouth and eyes but snorting something up my nose. Lurching back up above the surface, Rhea's arms already pulling at my jacket to get my head above it all. I threw up, vomiting out a stream of hot puke which mingled with what I was sitting in.

"Don't shoot!" I heard Rhea shout as she pulled me over to the side of the pipe, and as she helped me lean against it, I suddenly realised my arm and shoulder hurt like hell.

"Jesus, they fucking shot me!" I said, clamping my left hand over the gaping exit hole as best I could, trying not to think of infection. As the lights from the guards' torches bobbed over to us, I looked at Rhea and saw she'd been using her night vision binoculars, which now hung around her neck; if one of the troops had shone his torch into her eyes while she was wearing them, she'd probably have gone blind for a week.

"Stay where you are! Don't fucking move!" one of the troops said as the four of them came up to us. Three of them fanned out on our right as much as they could and kept us covered, their rifles trained on us, the little red dots hardly wavering from their resting places over our hearts. The leader shone his torch from one of us to the other. "Do you know what you've fucking done?" he said, asking the same question Ishmael had. "You've fucking killed the Godhead!"

Rhea and I glanced at each other and I knew she was thinking exactly the same thing I was: this guy had lost it. He was torn between avenging his beloved leader right here and now, and capturing us so that we could be put on trial by the authorities.

"You can't just kill us," Rhea said, turning to the guard. "You're gonna have to take us in." She stood away from the wall, her hands at her sides. "We're unarmed, and this man's been shot once already." I noticed with gratitude that only one of the guards moved to keep track of her, leaving the other two watching me.

"Keep fucking still," the commander of the team said,

bringing his rifle up to his shoulder. In the same movement, Rhea's left arm scythed up, accompanied by the metallic *shing!* of her machete sliding from its scabbard. The pipe was lit up for a moment as fire burst from the commander's rifle with a deafening CRACK! before he and Rhea went down, crashing together into the refuse and water, rolling around in the torch-light.

The guard who had followed Rhea's movement's stepped over and reached down with one hand into the churning water, trying to get a grip on something as the two who stood guard over me swapped glances. With a grunt, the first guard pulled someone up out of the water, someone who pushed a pistol under his chin and pulled the trigger, sending his skull and brains out of the top of his armoured helmet to spray against the ceiling of the pipe.

As Rhea turned, aiming the pistol at my two guards, they both spun and fired, lighting the pipe up again with rifle fire. One of them went down screaming, a great gout of blood jetting out from his neck, red and black in the strobing torch-light. Rhea vanished once again below the water level as I threw myself at the last man standing, forcing him down and under the sewage. I grabbed his rifle and twisted it, holding it in both hands and pushing down on it, not in an effort to strangle him but just to keep the bastard below the water, screaming as my shoulder bore my body weight. The light from his helmet and shoulder torches shone distinctly up through the dirty wa-ter and I caught glimpses of his face, his eyes bulging as much as his cheeks as he frantically pushed against me and the rifle, trying to lift me off him. He shook his head, eyes staring up at me as if he could see me through the same filthy, illuminated water until, with a last surge of bubbles, his mouth opened, air escaped and water rushed in. He bucked beneath me once, almost dislodging me, before simply going limp, a thin clot of blood trickling from his nose before mixing with the sewage and dispersing.

I stood, clutching at my shoulder, and looked around for Rhea but couldn't see anything; the torches of the troops were all underwater, or pointing up at the ceiling. I reached down into the water and tore one of them off the man I had just killed, then went back to my search.

"That better be you, Aitch," Rhea gasped as my torch-light fell on her a few moments later. She was as soaked and filthy as I was and had managed to pull herself up out of the water.

"It's me," I said, leaning next to her.

"Good, because I've lost that guard's pistol and my blade." I ran the torch over her, wincing when I found a ragged hole in the front of her coat which went all the way through to the back. It was hard to tell, even with the torch, but it was a safe bet that the dampness around it wasn't solely due to the water.

"We've got to get out of here," I said.

"No kidding?" Rhea said. "Fucker shot me, Aitch. Got me as I stabbed him."

"Come on, we've got to keep going. We stay here much longer, they'll send in more guards and we'll be fucked all over again." As best I could I stood up and pulled her with me, groaning with the weight, my shoulder complaining loudly. Our arms went round each other as we walked on, wading through all the shit, looking for a way out of this mess.

*

We came out near the Thames, not surprisingly. How long we walked I have no idea; our movement was marked only by the periodic necessity for either Rhea or me to pass out, throw up or do both at the same time. Three times I came to, choking on either my own vomit or something else that had lumps and had found its way into my nose and throat, pushed Rhea up and off me, waking her in the same moment.

We didn't talk, saving our breath and strength to walk through the darkness that seemed to become more and more complete with each step. Our only guide was the feel of the slurry against our legs, directing us forward, away from the church in Whitechapel where I had finally been relieved of that bloody Key. One time the floor just disappeared beneath us, sending us sliding down the steep pipe like kids on a fairground ride; the pair of us screamed, barrelling round and round in the pitch dark and the wet, not knowing if we were going to be spat out into some sort of grill or collection pit where we would be pinned or buried by the mass of filth that was speeding along with us. As it was, we came to a slow halt as the pipe became level again. With Rhea coughing up blood in my arms, we picked ourselves up and carried on walking.

It was night when we finally came to the end of the pipe. The city was quiet, with everyone tucked up in bed except for the skeleton staff at places like power stations or the emergency services. And the Church Police, of course. As we climbed out of the pipe, dropping the couple of feet to the muddy, grassy verge below us, we were startled by sirens. On the opposite side of the river, four or five vans — which looked to be the same kind that had chased Rhea, Hal and me on the day that seemed so long ago — roared along the road, chasing someone or something. We were too tired to care.

I sank almost up to my knees in the mud as I tried to take Rhea's weight and helped her stagger on to the firmer ground beyond the mouth of the pipe. The crap we had walked through, and on occasion almost swum through, drifted past our legs, cutting its filth-ridden way down the small embankment to mingle with the Thames, a dirty child being bathed by an uncaring parent.

With a few grunts and curses, I dragged myself out of the runnel and lay beside Rhea, propping my back against the wall from which the pipe emerged. Despite the cold December night air and the water freezing on my clothes, I could feel myself sweating. I pulled the side of my jacket away from my right shoulder, wincing at the sight of the huge hole, dark with blood, water and sewage smeared all around it.

Rhea coughed beside me, then threw up a huge amount of blood and bile, the steaming mess emptying into her lap as she sat, too tired to care about even turning her head.

"Christ, Aitch," she whispered, the words bubbling in the blood around her lips like miniature speech balloons. "Where the fuck . . . are we?"

"I don't know," I said truthfully, trying to wiggle the fingers on my right hand as I realised I couldn't feel them.

Then I had a sudden thought. "Do you remember being rescued by that Upper? From the holding station?"

"No."

"In the drive . . . in the car, as you came too, you said you loved me."

She laughed once, a single bark that turned into a cough.

"Was it me you were seeing?" For some reason, I had to know. As we sat there, sweating and bleeding in the cold, I needed an answer, as if I could feel time running out.

"Fucked . . . if I know . . . Aitch," she whispered into the night.

We sat in the dirt for a few minutes, watching the lights of London. I could hear the mess that the RAF bullets had made of her lungs as she breathed, and stopped myself from asking her about Corben and how she'd known her name. She was in no state to answer my questions. Hell, she was freelance; she'd probably worked with her in the past.

"What's . . . what's going to happen . . . now?" Her breathing was slow and ragged and, in the light from the street above and from the slim moon that peeked through the clouds, I could see she'd been hit more than once by the RAF. There were at least three bullet holes in her chest and, because of the close range at which she'd been shot and the explosive bullets they used, I could guarantee there were bloody great exit wounds in her back. I was lucky the shot I'd taken hadn't blown my arm right off. Looking down at the mass of tissue and sinew that still bled freely, though, I guess I hadn't been that lucky after all.

"I don't know." I said. "I think they'll make sure the Godhead carries on; Ishmael said he was nothing more now than a computer image on a screen, so the fact that he's dead isn't going to slow them down. Without Ishmael, though? I think they'll just set someone else up in his place. Stuff like that doesn't change. Like he said, the King never dies, no matter what fucker's on the throne." I sighed, my breath frosting in front of me, my soaking wet clothes seeming to wrap themselves tighter around me. "Still, if we get out of this, I know what I'm going to do. I'm through with stupid quests and metaphysical answers. I'm gonna kill every Downer and Upper I possibly can. If we can get rid of those fuckers and get people back in charge . . . I don't know, maybe we'll have a chance of sorting our shit out again. It's gonna take a while, but if we don't try and change stuff, the fuckers in charge'll just run us all into the ground time and time again. We've gotta try. We've got to. It's the only way out of this mess."

I sat and stared across the Thames at London spreading out into the night, thinking of the wall the Godhead and Ishmael had placed around this city and how good it would be to tear it down.

"We've got to try and get control back from them, Rhea," I said.

"I want . . . a fag," Rhea gasped, her hand flopping ineffectually at her coat pocket. I reached across and plucked out her lighter and two packs of Marlboros. One was open, the cardboard and the contents soaked through and useless; the other, though, was still wrapped in cellophane. I opened it and placed a cigarette between her blood-stained lips. It took only a moment's thought before I took one myself, weeks of denial going out the window.

"God bless Zippos," I said as, with only a half-dozen spins of the wheel, Rhea's lighter sprang to life, allowing me to light my cigarette before leaning over and offering it to her.

She sat, the cigarette dangling lifelessly from her lips, her gaze as cold as the air.

I clicked her lighter closed, sat back and smoked. I'd leave her after this fag, I thought, then I'd see about that wall.

Just as soon as I finished this cigarette.

Also available from RazorBlade Press:

razorblades
edited by Darren Floyd
ISBN: 0-9531468-0-4 £3.99 144pgs

Faith in the Flesh
by Tim Lebbon
ISBN: 0-9531468-4-7 £4.99/$9.00 144pgs

The Dreaming Pool
by Gary Greenwood
ISBN: 0-9531468-7-1 £4.99/$9.00 136pgs

Lonesome Roads
by Peter Crowther
ISBN: 0-9531468-1-2 £5.99/$13.99 154pgs

Hideous Progeny
edited by Brian Willis

ISBN 0-9531468 4 1 £6.99/$11.00 310pgs

The Ragchild
by Steve Lockley and Paul Lewis
ISBN 09531468 2-0 £4.99/$9.00 182 pgs

Hush
by Tim Lebbon and Gavin Williams
ISBN 09531468 5-5 $8.99/$15.00

coming soon:
Raw Nerve 8
edited by Brian Willis

For more information about RazorBlade Press visit our website at: **www.razorbladepress.com**